FAITH

.

FAITH IN EVERY FOOTSTEP

Wesley Banks

This is a work of fiction. All of the characters, organizations, and events portrayed in this novel either are products of the author's imagination or are used fictitiously. The novel includes fictitious elements in regard to the town of Whitehorse, Yukon, and the Yukon Quest in order to fit the story.

Faith In Every Footstep
Copyright © 2016 by Wesley Banks

First Edition: December 2016

ISBN 978-0-9861934-4-6 (e-book)
ISBN 978-0-9861934-5-3 (paperback)

Chasing Pace Publishing

FAITH IN EVERY FOOTSTEP

PROLOGUE

The woman dropped several eucalyptus leaves into the boiling water, and then a handful of dried chamomile flowers. Her hands moved with a delicate awareness around the dancing flames that licked and nipped below the cast-iron pot.

Smoke escaped from the woodstove through a tarry vertical exhaust. She opened the firebox and fed the orange blaze another log. Bits of white ash flaked across the pedestal and onto the floor.

Several feet to her left, the man lay silently on the bed. Every now and then his body shivered softly as his muscles tensed and relaxed. His eyes were still closed, and the fever sweats ran across his face, chest, and arms.

The younger of the two girls sitting nearby looked up at her mother. "Is he being healed in the Summerland?"

"The Summerland is a myth," the older sister said.

The woman squeezed drops of honey into the pot as she stirred it, and the room filled with the sweet minty scent of eucalyptol oil as steam from the tea began to rise. She turned to her teenage daughter. "Your great-grandfather was a master shaman for his people. Your father believes the teachings of the Inuit and the healing dreams that can take you to the Summerland. And I believe in your father."

Before the girl could protest any further, her father pushed himself up on both hands. The fever had broken, and his eyes focused on his wife.

"What is it?" the woman said.

He glanced down at his two daughters.

The woman rose and walked to her husband's bed. "Girls, go to your rooms please."

"But—" the youngest started.

"Now," the woman said sternly.

When the girls departed, the woman pulled the bedroom door shut, and the bottom rail struggled and scratched to a close.

Her husband whispered, "I have seen a great fire."

"And this troubles you?" she said.

"No, but standing in its midst..." He let the words trail off.

"Was what?"

His voice was clear but laced with hesitation, and he spoke in the old language of the Inuit. "Ataneq amaruq."

1

KYLE STOOD ON the bare ground, his head bathed in an ocean of frigid air, his feet heavy in last night's snow. In one hand he lifted the splitting maul over his shoulder, bits of bark and sap flinging from the now blunted end, while his other hand gripped a frostbit rope. The makeshift sled, weighed down by chunks of timber, creaked over the clean snow as he pulled it along the fence line.

The cabin in the distance moved deceptively as the endless plains of white smoke rose from the chimney. A drift of cool air rolled in over the mountains. It chewed through his Sherpa-lined jacket and slipped in between a loose layer of fleece and negative brushed base layer that hugged his skin. He stopped to zip his jacket up higher before the chill could cling to his body like a cold shower. The feeling was still new to him, and yet it was old.

Kyle opened the shed door and placed the axe, along with the freshly cut pieces of pine, in a worn groove along the left wall. The corrugated metal door clanged shut, and before he could turn around, he heard a familiar sound.

A low growl emanated from behind him. Every part of his body stiffened, except his neck, which he turned slightly to the left. The farthest part of his peripheral vision picked up the stark black coat. The cabin was nearly fifty feet across from the shed. He wouldn't make it there in time.

One. Kyle breathed out slowly through his mouth and in through his nose.

Two. He tensed the muscles in his hands, arms, legs, and core.

Three. Without warning, he pivoted on his left foot, pushing off with his right, and sprang at the animal. He was too slow though. Even at nineteen years old and in peak condition, he was not nearly as fast as a Carolina gray.

The animal jolted instantly, feinting away from Kyle and then flashing back at him.

Kyle wasn't defeated just yet though. He spun to his right as the black paws pierced the snow just inches away, and swiped back at the beast, clipping its front leg. Then he drove his weight forward and pushed the animal onto its side.

Kyle reached for the animal's neck, but again he was too slow, grasping nothing but air. He rolled onto his back but knew instantly he had made a mistake, exposing too much of his body.

In a blur the animal landed on top of him, and Kyle lay face to face with two cuspate fangs. He reached forward trying to find a safe handhold, but the fangs fell on each side. His hands gripped at clumps of fur along the animal's neck, soft but bristly in the cold.

Kyle baited the beast by relinquishing the grip in his right hand. He shifted his weight down and to the right, and just as the animal repositioned its paws, Kyle drove his left heel into the ground and flipped to his right. He meant to drive the animal into the snow, but he was left with nothing but bits of pitch-black fur between his hands.

Kyle pushed himself to all fours, but before he could stand, he found himself face to face with a pair of golden eyes. The moment the animal moved, Kyle knew it was over. He flinched and fell backward, but not fast enough. The wolflike creature stood atop him once again with a labyrinth of bared teeth.

But the snarl faded, and out came an elongated, soppy tongue. It tickled Kyle's neck and face, leaving droplets of slobber along the way.

"King." Kyle laughed. "Stop it. Stop it."

King had been Kyle's best friend since the day he discovered the rare breed of dog six years ago in the lowlands of South Carolina.

The booming sound of a passenger train interrupted their game. King and he both propped up on their left forearms and watched the train chug through the afternoon mist of the Yukon. Kyle looked over at King. His amber eyes, his thick black fur, his angular face and pricked ears. This was not just a dog, not just a wolf. This was a Carolina gray. And in less than twenty-four hours, Kyle hoped the world would know the breed as the greatest sled dog to ever live.

About twenty yards away the front door opened over a fresh layer of hoar frost, and Kyle looked down the length of his body to see Jane step onto the porch.

"You better get a move on. It's nearly three," she said.

Kyle stood and brushed a mixture of snow and fur off his jacket and fire-hose pants. The Alaskan sun still hung high above the tallest evergreens, but Jane was right. He was going to be late if he didn't head out soon. He breathed in and out, and his breath condensed visibly among the wintry air.

"Thank you," he said.

Jane shook her head. "Would you stop that nonsense?"

She was older, probably over three times Kyle's age, and he could see it now more than ever in the lines and creases across her face. But she was burly and hardened, and like the trees of the inland Yukon Territory, she held on to her youth in old age. She reminded him so much of Doc.

He had spent the better part of six months here. And without her none of this would have been possible. For the last few days, he had been trying to thank her for everything, but she wanted no part of it. Because thank you meant goodbye, and nobody wanted to say goodbye.

"I mean it," he said.

Jane let out an audible breath. "Finish up, and come get a little bit of soup before you head to town."

"You know this is the Musher's *Dinner*," he said.

"You need all the meat you can get on that bag of bones, 'specially since you're so stubborn. You'll run yourself ragged long before them dogs…" Her voice trailed off as the cabin door closed behind her.

Kyle let his eyes scan over the old miner's cabin. Two rows of silver sheet metal clung to the front of the roof, while the back made do with several pieces brick red with rust. The trim around the two windows on the side was painted the color of fresh biscuits, and just looking at the cabin made Kyle smile. Even though the Toyostove heater did absolutely nothing to prevent the bedrooms from turning into iceboxes. Even though the plumbing stopped working in January, and he had to clean dishes by heating water in the coffeemaker. Even though he yearned for the mild winters of South Carolina. He would miss this place.

The locomotive choked out several puffs of coal as the engineer announced the train's parting with a long pull of the horn.

Next to the shed, and across from the cabin, sat twelve more Carolina grays. Several howled from atop their snow kennels, matching the sound in both tone and cadence.

The dogs were used to the quiet comfort of Doc's barn, but they had spent all their downtime in the last six months tied up to wooden boxes, with saw-cut holes for front doors, just big enough to fit their curled-up bodies. The only thing that remained familiar was the scattered straw that most of them lay upon.

Kyle walked King over to the only vacant snow kennel and latched the silver chain to his collar. He had arranged the kennels in pairs, except for King's, which jutted out in front of the others. The layout mimicked that of the sled. Behind King was Story and Link, then Shyanne and Spirit, Hali and Sunshine, Giza and Gardens, Alexandria and Artemis, and finally Colossus and Olympia. Tails wagging and bodies stretched out shaking off the cold, each dog stood to greet him. Except Ria.

She lay still, her jet-black body in contrast to the snow, with her head resting at a slight angle across her front legs. Kyle knelt in front of her, and the frozen ground crunched under his right knee.

He didn't reach his hand out for her. He didn't speak. He just watched. His eyes traced down her neck and along her muscled shoulders, over the slick line where her hackles sometimes appeared, and around the sharp curves of her stifle and hock. Kyle rolled his wrist like he was reeling in a fish, and Ria leaned over onto her side. He slid his hand on the inside of her thigh to check her pulse. *Calm.*

"It's okay to be nervous," Kyle said.

Ria lifted her head and looked at him with two black eyes of infinite depth.

"I'm a little nervous about tomorrow too."

Ria plopped her head back down on several strands of straw.

Kyle ran his hand from her thigh up to her chest and let it rest there firmly for just a second. "Tomorrow will be here soon," he said. "Get some rest."

The train cried out one final time before the last car faded into the woods. A little boy stared out the window of the last passenger car, and on the brink of the world's toughest race, all Kyle Walker could think about was Bishopville, South Carolina, where this all started when he was just thirteen.

2

WHITEHORSE ALWAYS FELT strangely awkward to Kyle. Maybe it was the scene of a city overlooking the great Yukon River instead of nature alone. Maybe it was the fact that King wasn't by his side. Maybe it was just being in the most populated place in all the Yukon Territory. Whatever it was, he felt out of place.

The air was warmer in town, but thicker. Instead of the light touch of spruce or fir, the air tasted like a meringue of metal and oil and...chocolate. To his left was the Fudge Shack. He lifted his nose like he had seen King do so many times and inhaled one singular breath. The scent of caramel, sea salt, and sweet chocolate held him in place, but his eyes focused on another building behind the Fudge Shack—Yukon Dogs: International Dog Sled Museum. He looked at his watch: 5:57 p.m. He had an hour to kill.

Kyle didn't know the history of dog sledding like some of the other mushers. He didn't grow up here, and to be honest, he didn't much care about the facts. He learned to train dogs by training dogs, by living among them. By running with them through fields of switchgrass and lying beside them in exhaustion at the day's end. By breathing when they breathed. By paying attention to shadows and butterflies with unknowing curiosity and patience. It was only by unlearning everything his knowledge was founded on that he could then unearth their true nature.

In those same ways, he learned to sled and mush by sledding and mushing, albeit mostly over the dew-covered grass of Carolina hills. But his last six months in the Yukon Territory hadn't been much different, just whiter, colder, and wilder. The distant screams at night weren't the high-pitched cries of coyotes searching for food, but the sonorous howl of wolf packs signaling the movement of bison or elk. Beavers weren't busy building dams to fill the day—they were of a different ilk, preparing to fend off a free-ranging and famished bear. White-tailed deer didn't hop or scamper through fresh snow—instead moose and caribou sauntered confidently through their domain. He learned more about the wilds of Canada and Alaska by coming to terms with its savagery in the same way the dogs did. He didn't care about the facts because he didn't trust them.

Kyle wandered through the first floor of the museum without paying much attention, past the displays of Inuit and Eskimo sitting around a fire, past rows of bookcases decorated with figurines of dogs and mushers, laminated descriptions of each scene littered among them.

Halfway into the space, along a rising wall adjacent to the stairs, he reached an area dominated by old sleds and harnesses. The laminated paper signs read *Please Do Not Touch*, but Kyle couldn't help it. He reached down and ran his hand along the top rail of one sled, probably handcrafted with birch or hickory or some other hardy wood. From one knee he let his fingers glide across the runners that carried the sled over the snow, and then over the empty bed slats where the gear would normally reside. He could feel the knots where branches had been sawed

8

off and the discriminate patterns of bark that swirled like smooth sand. It looked like a carefully constructed basket, and many mushers referred to it as such.

"Excuse me, sir," said a voice from behind him.

Kyle banged his hand against one of the sled stanchions as he pulled away from the display. He spun. The girl was trying to hide her smile with her hand, but he could still see it within her keen green eyes. She crossed her left leg over her right. Her red hair was tucked into her parka.

"I'm sorry," she said. "I couldn't resist."

Kyle brushed a few pieces of burgundy carpet fuzz off his jeans and flexed his left hand. There was a long scratch from his first knuckle to his wrist. He held it up for her to see. "At least I played it cool."

"Oh my gosh. You're bleeding!" she said.

Kyle laughed. "I've had worse." He turned his hand over, palm up, revealing a scar that stretched from the base of his thumb down the outer edge of his radial bone for six or seven inches.

She reached out and grabbed his hand, yanking him forward a step.

He flinched. "Whoa, your hands are freezing."

"Oh, don't be a baby." She reached into her purse and pulled out a white plastic first-aid kit about the size of a wallet, and tore the top off an antiseptic packet.

Before he could protest, she grabbed his hand again, just above his wrist. The combination of the antiseptic wipe and her gelid fingers felt like a cool breeze tiptoeing across his skin.

"Girl Scout, huh?" he said.

"What?"

"The first-aid kid."

9

"Oh."

"It was a joke. I just...never mind."

She crumbled the wipe into a ball and stuffed it back into the used packet. Kyle noticed a faint blanket of freckles across the ridge of her nose when she gazed up at him.

"I'm Kyle, by the way."

"You don't remember me, do you?" she said.

They were the same pepper-green eyes and freckles from the Knik 200. "Umm..." Kyle's lips parted, but the words wouldn't come out.

"The vet check," she said. "You were that one rookie musher who kept insisting on being with each and every one of his dogs."

"But you weren't the vet that checked my dogs last week..."

"Not the Yukon. The Knik." She flipped open the first-aid kit again and pulled out a slender butterfly Band-Aid.

Kyle thought back. The Knik 200 was his first race in Alaska and one of the mandatory qualifiers for the Yukon. He remembered each and every step of the race. The banking turn at Horseman's Hollow that near capsized his sled. Curling up to King between checkpoints, in the snow at Old Woman. Shaking a multitude of calloused hands after winning the Best Kept Team award.

"I'm sorry. The vet checks are just so..."

"Chaotic?" she said.

"Yeah. I just don't like a lot of people handling my dogs. I'm not used to it really."

Kyle subconsciously ran his fingernail along the adhesive edge. "You didn't need to do that."

10

"Yeah, and next thing you know a certain musher is being forced out of the race because of a mild infection, or worse."

"Well, thank you," he said.

"It was kind of my fault anyways." She clamped the first-aid kit shut and placed it purposefully on the back left side of her purse.

Kyle watched her fingers' meticulous movements. "So can I get a do-over?"

She held his gaze for a moment. "I actually thought it was kind of endearing."

"What was?" Kyle said.

"The way you were with the dogs. It was…different."

"Different bad?"

"No."

"Different good?"

She smiled. "No. Just different."

Kyle wanted to keep talking to her but didn't know how to respond. So he said the only thing on his mind. "Do you want some fudge?"

Her smile turned into a laugh. "What?"

"Sorry. I walked past a fudge shop on my way in here, and I just can't get that smell out of my mind. I thought maybe you might want some? Or they probably have coffee or hot cocoa…"

"Sure," she said.

Kyle wasn't expecting her to answer so quickly. "Sure?"

"Oh, you were just being polite by asking me. I'm sorry. I didn't mean to be bothering you this whole time."

"No, no. No," Kyle said. He looked down at the stitching on her purse and replayed the sound of the first-aid kit snapping shut. It was a delicate force. "I want you to go. I was just…surprised."

They both stood in lingering silence. Kyle watched her with that same patience he had learned from King. She blinked in a single breath through her nose, and her lips flexed lightly as she breathed out. Her fingers glided along the leather strap of her purse until her thumb rested just beneath it, against her shoulder. She breathed in again, and her shoulders rose, only millimeters, but Kyle was drawn to her simple movements, her delicate force.

"Okay, let me get one more do-over." He held out his hand. "I'm Kyle."

She combed a tress of red hair behind her ears with her fingers and then shook his hand. "I'm Jenna." She smiled.

She couldn't see it, but Kyle bowed his heart before asking, "Jenna, could I take you to get some fudge?"

3

THEY WALKED ALONG Front Street, over the brick pavers near the Gwaandak Theatre and through the empty parking lot adjacent to the Yukon River. They carried bricks of fudge the size of their hands and wrapped in waxed tissue paper.

Jenna folded back the waxed paper and broke off a chunk.

"Good?" Kyle asked.

Jenna nodded, her mouth full of rocky road fudge. She held it out. "Want some?"

"No, I don't like marshmallows," Kyle said.

Jenna stopped walking. "Who doesn't like marshmallows? How is that even a thing? That's like not liking...ice cream."

Kyle averted his eyes from hers and wiped, on the wrapping, a dab of fudge that clung to his thumb.

"Oh. My. Gosh. You don't like ice cream?"

"It's just too cold, and the consistency bothers me."

"You're about to take a group of dogs on the toughest race in the world through weather that can dip below negative fifty degrees, and ice cream is too cold?"

Kyle grinned. "Well, yeah. I mean, I could sled over a river of frozen ice cream. I just don't want to eat it."

Jenna started walking again. "Okay, now I'm dreaming of a river of ice cream. Maybe mint chocolate chip or cookie dough. Yeah, definitely cookie dough."

"You want some of mine?" Kyle said.

Jenna pointed at his sprinkle- and M&M-covered chocolate fudge. "No thanks. I graduated kindergarten."

"All right. Suit yourself. These sprinkles are deeeliiiiicious." Kyle kicked at a loose paver near the yellow handicap ramp as they passed the Old Fire House and turned left onto Main Street. Crisp and bushy pink, purple, and white silk petunias shivered from a westerly wind, their plastic pots clicking against the green light poles from which they hung.

"So, did you grow up here?" Kyle asked.

Jenna nodded as she finished off another bite of rocky road fudge. "Born and raised," she said. "Even went to University of Alaska Fairbanks."

"And you went to vet school?"

"Graduated last summer."

Kyle did the math in his head. That put her at least a few years older than him. "How did you get involved in the sled dog side of it?"

"My dad's a vet. He used to take me to the races when I was a kid, and it's just something I've always wanted to do. What about you?"

"Nope, I'm not a vet."

Jenna rolled her eyes. "You know what I mean. Where are you from? How'd you get into mushing? Do you have any other deep, dark secrets besides hating marshmallows and ice cream?"

"Born in raised in the blue hills of Bishopville, South Carolina. Just kind of started running the dogs. And, maybe."

14

"The hills are actually blue?" she said.

"You get out about as often as I do." He laughed.

"So they're not blue?"

"Technically, no. But the thousands, or hundreds of thousands, of trees that line the mountains give off something called isoprene, which mixes with the atmosphere to refract a sort of bluish hazy light."

"That's actually really cool," Jenna said.

"Yeah, it's not bad."

"What about your parents?" she asked. "Was your dad a musher?"

"I don't know," he said.

Jenna scrunched up her nose. "What do you mean?"

Kyle crumpled the waxed paper and tossed it in a trash can as they stepped off the sidewalk that poured into an unfinished lane of gravel. In front of them a large plastic sign flapped in the wind. It covered the top two stories of the Northern Light Hotel, and in huge cursive letters read *Looking for Love Again*.

Kyle pointed toward the hotel, at an enormous mural that covered the concrete wall. "What's that?"

"That? That is the legend of Kishkumen."

Kyle crossed the street and walked until he stood just a few feet away from the painting. It was probably five feet tall and ten feet wide. The scene was drawn with such detail that it almost looked lifelike. He reached out and ran his hand along the chapped and choppy concrete.

On the left side was a single white wolf lying in the snow. To the right and in the distance was a black wolf running toward her. His fur was ruffled and craggy, but his eyes were focused and fierce. Above him the sun was rising, and light-bent rays shone just a few paces behind his outstretched legs.

15

Jenna stood next to Kyle. "The legend speaks of a white wolf named Larka, who was mortally wounded. Her mate, Kishkumen, was heartbroken, until one night the moon came to him. The moon told him of an ancient magic. That the one who can outrun the sun holds power over the sway of death. Kishkumen waited until just before dawn the following morning, and at first light he began to run. The legend says that he ran across the entire earth in a single day."

"Did he outrun the sun?"

"He did. But in doing so, it killed him."

"So he didn't save Larka?" Kyle said, still staring at the stark image before him.

"It depends on how you look at it," Jenna said. She put her left hand on his shoulder and pointed with her right. "You see those two stars?"

Kyle looked at two crisscrossed objects hanging in the sky above the white wolf. He nodded.

"When Kishkumen died, he joined Larka in the sky, and forever they stand together, side by side."

Jenna's watch vibrated, and she looked down at the alarm. "Come on," she said. "We gotta go."

Kyle heard the words, but they felt distant and drowned out. Not by the cars driving down Front Street. Not by the raucous voices from the bar on the corner. Not by the sounds of the vibrant colors on the wall in front of him. No, it was the cacophony of palpitations from his very heart.

It beat to the rhythm of the story, to the rhythm of Kishkumen striding across the earth with every ember of his being. And it scared him.

"Kyle," Jenna said again. "We're going to be late."

Kyle's hands shifted in his pockets, but his focus refused to abandon the shining stars of Kishkumen and Larka in the sky.

Jenna leaned toward Kyle and mirrored him. Hands in pockets, her right foot planted alongside his left. He could sense her eyes search the space on the mural that his so intently held.

"What are we looking at?" she whispered.

He smiled down at her, and there they were, the same green eyes from the dog sled museum, surrounded by a sparse garden of freckles. The same green eyes from the Knik 200.

She crossed her arms. "Don't tell me you're ready to chance the wilds of Alaska on sled but you're scared of a little dinner."

"I'm not scared. I'm just..."

"Scared?" she joked.

"I'm not scared," he said walking past her. "At least, not of them."

Kyle paused before crossing the street. He looked to his right and then his left. A dark gray hatchback was parked along the curb, covered in a crust of ice, except for the back window that had been scraped clean. The sun flew down at just the right angle, and Kyle saw his reflection staring back at him. He didn't fear the unshakeable cold or the ever-changing elements. He didn't fear the other mushers or worry about the ability of his dogs. Lack of food, lack of sleep, or the loneliness of the trail. They were nothing more than a passing thought. But the man in the glass staring back at him. The man that would be with him to the clear end. He was the most dangerous test.

4

THE MUSHER'S DINNER was at a surprisingly casual-looking place called Pine Tavern. Red, green, and yellow letters were lit up on a sign outside that read *Friday RIBS*.

Kyle and Jenna made their way across the gravel parking lot that was already spilling out onto the frontage road with cars. He held the door open for Jenna, and when they stepped inside, it was more a hole in the wall than a restaurant.

High-top laminate tables spread across the floor, adorned by duct-taped faux leather chairs and the occasional barstool. The ceiling was blanketed by black-and-white tile in a pattern Kyle couldn't discern. A full-service bar lined the far end, equipped with shelves of endless brown liquor.

Family, friends, and other fans poured in through another door opposite Kyle, filling up tables in the back. Some fans were the winners of auctioned-off dinners, for the meeting of the mushers.

"Mr. Walker," a woman with a clipboard said, "you're at table one with Abbie Turner, Martin Laroux, and Ewan Harbinson." She pointed across the room at a table sitting directly in front of the podium.

He looked over at Jenna, but she was already walking in the opposite direction. Something within Kyle moved, and he found his hand around Jenna's arm, pulling her away from the crowd near an empty bar top attached to the wall with frost-filled windows.

Kyle let go of her arm, stuffed his hands back in his pockets, and leaned against one of the circle-top stools.

"Umm, Kyle...what are we doing?" Jenna said.

She was closer to him than she had been before. The fabric of her jeans brushed against his legs, and his eyes focused on that one spot of contact. "I just wanted to know if you...really liked the fudge?"

"You wanted to know if I *really* liked the fudge?"

"Yeah, I mean, I didn't want you to have bad fudge."

Jenna repeated his words again. "You didn't want me to have bad fudge?"

"Well..." Kyle started.

"Stop," Jenna said, lightly grasping his arms. "Look at me."

He did, and the strands of emerald in her eyes stole every bit of his breath.

"I *really* liked the fudge," Jenna said. "Did you?"

Kyle nodded.

"Is that a yes?" Jenna asked.

Kyle smiled as he spoke. "Yes."

She let her hands fall, and her fingers came to a rest on his knees as she leaned in. "Good."

Another woman with cropped brown hair called Jenna's name. She pushed away from him, mouthed the word *relax*, and winked.

Kyle made his way to table one, but the restaurant was crowded and loud. He accidentally bumped the back of another chair. The bearded musher everyone called "Milkshake" turned around. The man didn't say anything, just smiled an ear-to-ear grin. Kyle nodded in response.

When he finally reached the table, the only seat left was between Abbie and Ewan. He recognized Abbie from other races, and he'd seen Ewan on TV, magazines, and just about anywhere else that mentioned dog sledding in the past few years. Kyle moved to pull the chair out, but Ewan grabbed it.

"Seat's taken."

Kyle looked back toward the lady at the front door. "I was told table one."

"This table's for mushers. You can go have a seat with some of the others in the back."

"Oh, stope bayin' an ass," Martin said with a thick French accent. Kyle remembered that same accent from trails of the Knik. It was both memorable and hilarious to hear Martin shout a mix of French and English commands to his team.

"Forgive him," Abbie said. "He's always like this."

Ewan released the chair, and Kyle sat down.

Abbie held out her hand. "I'm Abbie."

Kyle shook her hand. "I know. I saw your finish last year. You got the Dawson Award, right?"

"Yeah, and over the next few checkpoints I had to drop eight dogs to injury, and basket another. Almost ended up last place because of it."

"But coming in with seven dogs like that at the end. That was incredible." Kyle reached for the pitcher of water and poured it from the side so that his cup filled mostly with ice.

"Aye," Martin said from across the table. "'Twas."

"Injuring ten dogs in one single race. Absolutely incredible," Ewan spat. He swallowed the last of his water and grabbed the pitcher just as Kyle sat it down.

"Seriously, we really do ignore him," Abbie said.

Kyle watched as Ewan thumbed his full glass of water. He'd heard about Ewan, read about him. He was a three-time winner of the Yukon, and current reigning champion.

"So, ho you bean, keed?" Martin said. They'd chatted once briefly over some soup at one of the Knik checkpoints. "Those last toe races wear preety toof."

Martin was alluding to the fact that Kyle had finished in the bottom five in both races. He had used the Knik 200 to steadily increase the team's pace, and the Race to the Sky 350 for extra elevation training. Kyle wouldn't bother to explain that those races served different purposes for him and his dogs, neither of which was about winning. The Yukon would be different, but he just nodded and agreed. "Yeah, they were pretty bad. My dogs are still learning though."

Ewan guffawed, drawing attention from the table next to them. "You think those were 'pretty bad'?" He stood up and placed his hands on the table. "You need run back to the Carolinas while you still can, and take those abominations you call dogs with you."

Kyle jumped up and stepped to within inches of Ewan. He could see the week-old stubble that lined his jaw and smell the bacon, which he's probably had for breakfast, on his breath. Kyle's right hand tightened around the chair behind him. He was pretty confident he could swing it from a dead rest across Ewan's snickering smile. If he had stood there a second longer, he probably would have, but a cool hand ran over the top of his.

"Excuse me," Jenna said. "Could I just borrow Mr. Walker for a second?"

"That would probably be a good idea," Abbie said.

Jenna's hand wrapped around Kyle's, and she pulled him back toward her table. Kyle looked down at her hand leading his. Their fingers weren't interlocked. Her thumb wasn't tracing small circles across his. It probably wasn't intimate to her at all, and yet it was all he could think about. He was so fixated on it that he nearly knocked her over when she stopped at the back of the restaurant.

She let go of his hand and took a step back.

"Sorry," he said, but as he looked at her, he couldn't help but smile.

"Do you have any idea who that..." Jenna stopped midsentence. "What's so funny?"

Kyle ran his hand up and down the back of his head, but he couldn't think of anything except the truth. "You were holding my hand."

Jenna balked. "And that's...funny?"

"No, I wasn't laughing. I was just smiling."

"Why?"

"Why what?" he said.

"Why were you smiling?"

Kyle reached his hand behind his head again and ran his fingers through his hair. In the last six months, it had grown a lot longer than he was used to. "I don't know..."

Jenna crossed her arms.

"It just made me happy," he said.

Jenna bit her bottom lip, clearly fighting back a smile. She took a step closer and spoke. "You think you can make it the rest of the night without getting into trouble?" Her words were soft and steady.

"But I didn't—"

Jenna raised her eyebrows and tilted her head.

22

"Yes, Mom," Kyle said.

The distinct sound of someone tapping on a microphone echoed throughout the room, and the shuffle of voices behind them settled. The rap and scratch of the wooden chairs dissipated, and the clang of silverware and glasses rang out as they came to a rest.

Kyle spun to face the stage.

An older gentleman, with a deep-gray beard and bare splotches on his cheeks, stepped to the podium.

"It's time for the drawing of bibs," Kyle said as he turned back to Jenna—but she was already walking back to her table.

* * *

Kyle found the seating at his table had changed when he returned. Ewan was sandwiched between Martin and Abbie, leaving the only open seat across from Ewan. Kyle sat down, ignoring Ewan and pivoting his chair so he could focus instead on the grizzly-looking man at the podium, to the left of the table.

The man's voice belied his looks, leaking out nasally toned words and a sniffle between each sentence. "Today we're here to kick off the 2003 Yukon Quest, and wish all of the teams well. We also want to acknowledge how hard all twenty-nine of these mushers have worked, including the dogs, who have become the true heroes of this race. While other professional athletes receive their sport with the cozy compliance of the rink, court, or field, your arena is over one thousand miles of grueling landscape where even mighty rivers and mountains bow down to the frozen tundra and unyielding winds. We truly are in awe of the feat that lies before you."

Several people hooted and hollered. Kyle raised his glass with some of the others at the table and looked around the room. Even the worst of them here would be formidable on the trails.

"At this point I'd like to ask Mr. Cody Stratham to come up on stage for the drawing of the bibs."

The room broke out in applause. Kyle looked back as Milkshake rose from his seat, thrust his glass stein in the air, and let out a "Woooohooooo!" The room erupted again, some laughing and others joining in with more hooting and hollering.

Mr. Stratham took to stage with a bright pink-and-green-striped bunny boot covered in different-sized rhinestones. He struggled to adjust the microphone down to his height and nearly dropped the boot, but recovered by pinning it between his belly, which bowed out in front of him, and the podium. Kyle didn't know how it all started, but it had become tradition to draw names from it.

The man held the boot in the air and spoke into the microphone. "I know this is what you're all here for, so without further ado, drawing first, from Two Rivers, and last year's champion, Ewan Harbinson."

Again the room filled with claps as Ewan clambered to the stage. He reached his hand into the sparkling boot, pulled out a piece of white paper folded in half, and handed it back to Mr. Stratham. "Mr. Harbinson will be going out twelfth!"

Mr. Stratham handed Ewan the microphone. It was customary for the musher to say a few words, but Ewan pushed the microphone away and stomped back to his seat.

The next twenty minutes went much the same, except all the other mushers elected to speak for a couple minutes. Some thanked their families, others their dogs. Milkshake thanked

24

everyone in the room, to which they all cheered, and Martin spoke in his broken English for over five minutes. Without the help of Abbie, he might have never left the stage. He got lucky number seven, and he just kept saying how happy he was to be here.

Kyle's turn finally arrived. "Please welcome Mr. Kyle Walker to the stage, drawing twenty-seventh." Kyle didn't much care for any of the cheers and whistles, even if one of them was Jenna. He'd rather be back home with the dogs, preparing for tomorrow, but he knew tradition was important, so he honored it.

Only three numbers were left by the time his hand slipped into the polyfiber boot. He felt the course cellulose and pinched the paper between his fingers.

"Number thirteen," Mr. Stratham said.

He would be going out behind Ewan "the Hammer" Harbinson.

5

KYLE TURNED the two-tone Ford—which he had driven from South Carolina six months ago—over a patch of muddied snow, and the truck whined like an empty ice machine. As he slowed down, the steering wheel felt more like a pressurized locking wheel on a submarine.

He pulled the truck onto a pair of old scaffolding boards that he'd set down after getting stuck several times, and the yellow haze of the headlights washed over Jane's cabin. Kyle was always amazed how quiet the Yukon could be. His footsteps alone echoed through the night like crumpling paper.

He slogged his way past the shed and over to the thirteen square igloos that each of the dogs had learned to call home. Except, all of the dogs were gone.

Kyle shook his head and smiled in the evening light. "I can't believe her."

When he opened the door to the cabin, King nearly knocked him over. On his hind legs, King's paws reached Kyle's shoulders, and the padded balls of King's feet contracted and wrapped behind Kyle's back.

Jane sat in her rocking chair by the stove, head buried in a book of crossword puzzles. "Don't look at me like that," she said from below her reading glasses.

"I thought…"

Jane sat her puzzle book down and looked up at Kyle. "You thought nothin'. Them dogs have spent the last five or six months out in the cold, and ain't no harm in givin' them a warm night inside."

It was in the teens outside and probably the forties in the cabin. Not exactly warm, but Kyle knew this wasn't an argument he would win.

"So where are the others?" Kyle said. He watched Jane fight back a grin as she picked her crossword book back up. "You didn't."

Kyle walked down the short hallway and swung open the door to his room. Silent, and stacked like kittens on his bed and floor, were twelve Carolina grays. Not a one of them moved as he stared them down. The markings above their eyes twitched left and right like children trying to hide some blatant yet mischievous deed.

Link waddled over, ears pressed against his head, his butt outwagging his tail. He slipped his head between Kyle's legs and just stood there.

"You know she spoils you guys. You're lucky you're all not fat little sheepdogs by now."

At the sound of his voice, Story darted toward him and bumped Link out of the way.

"Story," Kyle said sternly. "We don't do that."

The black-and-white dog stood on her hind legs and pivoted until her back was against Kyle. He wrapped his arms around the dog, letting her paws rest atop his folded arms. He made the mistake of looking down, and her tongue shot out at his face.

"You're going to get it now!" he said. She squirmed free and jumped onto the bed, but Kyle lunged after her. In a matter of minutes, the room was afresh with white, black, and ginger hair.

Kyle wrestled with eleven of the dogs until Story got a little too rambunctious. King lashed out at her in an instant, and she darted across the room.

"King!" Kyle called. He was ready to scold the dog, until he saw Ria. She was curled up behind King. Her eyes flicked across the room, but her body lay motionless, except the rise and fall of her breath.

Kyle left several of the dogs still playing on the bed and knelt beside her. He placed his right hand over her shoulder and let it stay there for two to three breaths, then moved it down over her lungs, heart, stomach, liver, and spleen, palpitating lightly between breaths as he went. Everything was fine. He checked her eyes, nose, ears, feet, and tail. Nothing.

And then as if one of the other dogs had given her a silent command, she rose to her feet and jumped into the fray that used to be a bed. She raced around the corners of the mattress and flung herself back at Kyle. He fell onto his back as her tongue assaulted him. He dug his hands into the thick fur around her neck and rubbed his fingers in small circles against her skin.

"That's my girl," Kyle said. "That's my girl."

The clang of mechanical plastic filled the house, and Kyle heard Jane answer the phone in the other room.

"I was wondering if you'd call…Yes, he is… Hold on. Let me get him…"

He shut all the dogs except King in the room and walked out to the kitchen.

"Oh, here he is." Jane handed Kyle the phone.

"Hello," Kyle said. He heard Doc's voice on the other end and looked down at his watch. It was past midnight in Bishopville.

"You ready for tomorrow?" Doc said.

"Yeah, I am."

"What about the dogs?" Doc said.

Kyle walked back to the room and cracked open the door where the dogs were sprawled across his room, and twelve pairs of eyes focused on him. "They're...good."

"You want to try that again?" Doc said.

"They're good," Kyle said. "Ria was just acting kind of weird today."

"Dehydrated?" Doc asked.

"No, I checked."

"She holding food down?"

"Yeah, no problems there."

"What about the other end?"

"Stool has been normal," Kyle said.

"Heart and lungs?"

"Checked both. Both were normal. But..."

"But?"

Kyle instinctively dropped his hand to King, who was following him around the house as he talked. "She was shaking earlier."

Kyle could picture Doc scratching his bristly beard, and it came through like static. "Bring her in for the night. Give her some Benadryl. Check her in the morning. My guess is she'll be right as rain."

"All right," Kyle said, silent for a moment.

"You still there?"

29

"Yeah, umm, I'm...scared."

"I know," Doc said. "I'd be more worried if you weren't. Everything worth doing starts with being a little scared. But trust yourself. And if you can't, trust King. Now go get some rest, and let me talk to Jane for a second."

"Aunt Jane," Kyle yelled.

She came scurrying out of her room. He handed the phone back to Jane and walked across the cabin to a window that looked out to the railroad tracks.

* * *

"Yes," Jane said as she huddled over the phone. It was nice to hear her brother's voice more often lately, even if was mostly from just passing the phone to Kyle. "I am," she said. "He is... I know... He has been... That too." She paused. "Henry," she said, using Doc's first name, "I've been out here the last thirty years, and I still don't understand any of this. I'm worried... No, the dogs are fine... No, he's fine physically... I know they're prepared... It's just, he's chasing something, Henry... Okay... I love you."

She sat the phone down on the receiver and watched Kyle's hand fall instinctively to King's head as the dog sat beside him. King watched Kyle and waited.

She repeated Doc's words in her head.

He's chasing what every man chases...himself.

6

BY THE TIME Kyle arrived in town, race crews had been out for hours, brushing and packing down the opening trail. Several snow blowers were still intermittently running to keep the starting area packed with fresh snow, but even they were drowned out by a crowd of people flooding Whitehorse.

A yellow sign with blue lettering flapped overhead against two aluminum poles, marking the starting line. Front Street, along the Yukon River, was completely shut down, and people flooded in to create a natural barrier for miles down the street. Staff members garbed in reflective orange-and-yellow construction vests helped keep the starting chute straight and clear.

A young reporter with curly blond hair stood several feet from Kyle's team. Hanging from his neck was a fancy-looking camera and a laminated card with the name *HUEY* printed in all caps. He gripped a notepad in his right hand, and it seemed as though he couldn't decide whether taking a picture or taking notes was more important.

From fifty yards behind the starting line, Kyle watched as several handlers and volunteers helped Ewan straighten out his dogs. Airplanes and HAM radio operators were already monitoring the progress of the first eleven teams, and within the next minute, Ewan would make twelve. Two minutes after that, Kyle would be thirteen.

Kyle looked around at the scene that surrounded him. He breathed it in. Every cheer, every shout, every gloved clap. Every bark, every yip, every anxious lunge. The electrical hum of the buildings, the elastic creak from the sled and rigging. His shoulders tensed. His ears overflowed with the noise. And then he breathed it all out. A cold chill swept through his body, and for the moment he relaxed.

From behind him came an unexpected voice. "You ready?"

"I thought you were supposed to be at the Braeburn checkpoint?" he said.

She winked. "Trying to get rid of me already?"

"No, I just…"

"Don't worry," she said. "I have a ride to Braeburn in a few. Just wanted to check on the dogs one last time."

She walked past him toward his dogs, where four volunteers were already standing, trying their best to keep the Carolina grays calm. Jenna passed Colossus, who looked more like a baby black bear, and his sled mate, Olympia, first. Their coats were thick, their forms commanding, their poise pacific. They were Kyle's wheel dogs. When the sled got stuck in the trace or found a tree well, some of the other dogs might be distracted, but good wheel dogs couldn't be. They were the ignition, the power that propelled the team.

Jenna ran her hand over Olympia's ginger fur as she passed. Giza and Gardens were next, followed by Artemis, Ria, Hali, Sunshine, Spirit, and Shyanne.

Giza and Gardens looked similar to Colossus in color, but were both female. They stood with ease and grace. Artemis was one of the oldest dogs in the pack at nine years, while

Alexandria, or Ria, as Kyle often called her, was just shy of two. She was young, but she was natural. Hali was a dark rich black, while Sunshine was mostly white with black spots that resembled hand-drawn clouds. Spirit was raven-like with a white triangle upside down on her chest, and Shyanne was similar to Sunshine, covered in white and dappled with coal-black spots. These were the team dogs. If Colossus and Olympia were the ignition, then these dogs were the fuel.

Three dogs remained. Jenna stopped next to one and knelt on one knee. She ran her fingers around his floppy ears, but even she couldn't stay his attention. His head jerked left and then right. But not at the screaming cheers or the flashing cameras. For Link it was much simpler. He lunged forward and nipped at the air, just missing a fitful fly. He loved chasing bugs.

The younger dog next to Link interrupted his fun. She rammed her head into his side and bit at his legs. Story was a perfect picture of energy and exuberance.

Other mushers might have found them an odd pairing, but Kyle had discovered that together, they were unmatched. They were his swing dogs. When the team turned together, it was because of Story and Link. They had to be more alert and aware than the team dogs or wheel dogs. They had to be incredibly quick, not only with their feet, but with their minds.

But even they paled in comparison to King.

Jenna stood up and looked at King.

Kyle had not paired King with another dog, and he stood alone as a single lead. Single leads in a race like the Yukon Quest were rare because it was an instant handicap to start with one less dog.

Unless that dog was King.

He was the size of Colossus, with the suddenness of Story. The first joint of his legs sat several inches below his chest, articulating his long legs. His chest and hips were narrower than that of a Husky, so he sacrificed some of their raw power but made up for it with pure speed.

Kyle observed King carefully as he gazed back at Jenna with unpredictable amber eyes, his coat the color of shadows. Without warning, he arched his neck and let out a sonorous and slow howl.

Several of the team joined in, while others bayed and barked. They were ready. They were ready.

"Well?" Kyle said as Jenna meandered back toward him, her eyes scanning each dog one last time.

"They look good," she said. "I think they're anxious to get going."

As she said that, Ewan's sled pulled away from the starting line. From behind his sled, Kyle relaxed the brake just enough for the excitement of the dogs to pull the sled forward. He was up.

Jenna walked alongside Kyle and spoke with a serious tone. "One more thing. Rely on your own good judgment. Check weather reports before the race and at checkpoints when possible. Use the known speed of your dog team to estimate distances. A GPS is a tool that can fail. And above all else..." Jenna paused.

"Above all else?" Kyle said.

She reached into her coat pocket and pulled out a bifold brochure about the Yukon Quest. "Above all else know your own team—their abilities, attitudes, and individual strengths."

"I'm going to pretend you didn't just read from the event brochure," Kyle said.

"What? That's good advice! Why else do you think they put it in the brochure?"

A loudspeaker came on, and a metallic voice announced, "Running thirteenth, behind our defending champion, is rookie musher Kyle Walker. Give him and his dogs a hand."

"Be careful," Jenna said.

Kyle held her eyes for a moment, then looked forward and at the nearly two hundred pounds of gear packed in the sled. He scanned over each of the thirteen dogs one last time, until his view rested on King alone. The dog shook his head left and right. He bent down and scented the ground where Ewan's team had just stood, and then he looked back at Kyle for the command.

"King!" Kyle yelled.

Story lunged forward, Ria barked, and Colossus strained against his harness.

"Hike!"

7

THE YUKON QUEST recognized that not knowing the trail was a distinct disadvantage for rookies. But Kyle had studied every inch of the trail via weather reports, maps, previous races, books, videos—and practice runs with his team. He knew each turn from Whitehorse to Fairbanks by heart. He recalled that King Solomon's Dome was the highest mountain pass, but Eagle was the steepest and most remote. He could visualize several distant cabins near Circle City, and he could even hear the silent streams near Scroggie Creek and Finger Lakes. Yet still he found himself searching out the reflective markers that lined the trail.

The team approached a cluster of evergreens hiding the left boundary marker. "Gee, gee, gee!" Kyle yelled. He bent his knees and leaned to the right as the Carolina grays quickly corrected course, veering back to the trail. Kyle lifted his left boot off the footboards and let it skate over the frosty ground. "Good girl, Story. Good job, Link."

Ria bayed and yipped into the oncoming breeze.

"You too, Ria. Good girl."

Kyle watched the dogs as they moved over the bare tundra. King's tongue hung out the left side of his mouth as he ran, his eyes scanning the trail ahead. Story ran next to Link but several steps ahead, her tug line held taut. Sunshine's head was covered in clumps of ice and snow, hiding her black mask, and Ria kept looking over to the older, more experienced Artemis. Ria was brilliant in every aspect of the word. She floated over the snow and accelerated through turns, like a cloudburst. But she was still young and not as surefooted as the others.

The world so settled and hushed around them that Kyle could hear every step the dogs took, every deep breath or huff. The snow was a few days old, which left the trail flat and fast. He was pushing them harder than the previous two races, which were nothing more than an acclimation. This race was different. It was a test, a platform to show the world that the Carolina gray was the greatest dog breed. But it wasn't just a test for the dogs. It was also a trial of who he was as a musher, and who he was as Kyle Walker. And he couldn't live with anything less than his best.

He watched the cascade of green leaves pass as they cruised through a tunnel of bent blue spruce and patches of hemlock. The sled hit a thick spool of snow, and the runners and railings shook. He peered down at the watch that was strapped to the driver's bow, where his hands rested. They had been on the trail for almost ten hours and had traveled nearly a hundred miles. The temperature dipped below zero for the first time as dusk settled in.

Kyle let out a deep breath and tried to relax his shoulders, which he had been subconsciously holding tense. He rolled his neck left and back right in a semicircle and stretched his arms over his head one at a time. They'd only stopped once in the first ten hours, just brief enough for a water break and some dried elk jerky.

Braeburn, the first checkpoint, was fast approaching, and while Kyle hadn't expected to catch Ewan on the first day, he was a little unnerved to not have seen a single team. The feeling quickly faded as the wind lifted the faint but familiar sounds of voices and camera clicks.

A few more yards and the wilderness unfolded into Braeburn. Ewan's sled was stopped, his hook brake embedded into the snow, and his dogs resting on small piles of straw. He looked over at Kyle as he tried to straighten out the gangline so he could unclip the tug line that connected to each dog's harness. This would leave just their neck lines attached so the dogs would be able to turn around and get comfortable on their makeshift beds.

Several journalists stepped into Kyle's line of sight, their questions and camera flashes breaking up the beaming looks between mushers.

Kyle wanted to push straight through the checkpoint, to ignore the initial crowds of volunteers, handlers, and reporters that would die out in the more remote parts of the race. Even though his dogs needed some rest. Even though they needed water. Even with the temperature dropping and the fact that he needed to get the windproof fleece-lined coats on several of the short-haired dogs—Link, Hali, Artemis, and Ria. Even knowing all that, the site of Ewan's sled urged Kyle to keep going. There would be risks to take in this race, but this wasn't one of them.

A mandatory four-hour layover was required either at Braeburn or at the next checkpoint. And Kyle wanted to get it over with.

The checkpoint contained the Braeburn Lodge, a former roadhouse on the Dawson Overland Trail. Kyle knew it was famous for its plate-sized cinnamon rolls that many of the mushers loved.

He let his dogs hike past Ewan's sled to where a couple volunteer handlers were waving him in. A shallow trench, two to three feet deep, had been dug in the snow, the top shelf of the trench lined with bales of hay for the dogs to rest in without losing any more energy or heat.

The sled slowed to a near stop, and one handler started to shake loose some of the straw around the dogs' feet.

From behind the sled, Kyle put his hand up, and the man stopped. He must have heard the same rumors as Jenna: "crazy rookie musher."

The handler pointed to a large bucket and said, his voice tinged with indignation, "There's water here for the dogs."

Kyle shook his head as the man walked away, more at his thoughts than at the helping hand. *They don't understand. One wrong step and he could break a dog's toe, or worse, slip and fall on a dog, bruising a leg, neck, or back.* It just wasn't worth the risk.

Kyle tossed out two snow hooks, one connected to each end of the gangline, so the dogs could stretch out in a line. He grabbed the silver bowls stacked by the water and set one in front of each dog. Then he grabbed the five-gallon bucket and poured about a pint into each with a massive aluminum ladle.

The dogs didn't lap at the water calmly, like after a quick game of catch in the backyard. They bit at with voracity, as if it were the last bit of water on earth. Like the other dogs in the Yukon Quest, Kyle's Carolina grays utilized between six and twelve thousand calories every twenty-four hours, depending on temperatures, and it took approximately one gallon of water per dog, per day to utilize those calories.

Kyle walked between them and pushed the straw around, making sure the dogs actually lay on it. The dogs with fuller coats—King, Colossus, and Giza—were overheated and preferred the cool touch of snow against their fur. But heat was a valuable commodity in the Yukon Territory, and wasting it wasn't wise. Kyle started to check each dogs' feet and recalled the words from one of the books he'd read: *Watch and care for your dogs' feet. As go the feet—so goes the dog.*

Doc had taught him something called "counting to ten." *One, two, three, four*—Kyle checked each of the digital pads. *Five, six, seven*—he examined the dew pad, metacarpal pad, and carpal pad. *Eight, nine, ten*—for three seconds he ran his fingers between each of the claws.

Colossus, Olympia, and Artemis all looked great, but as he finished examining Ria, he noticed a subtle tremor in her paw. She pulled her paw away, but Kyle reached out for it again and rubbed his hand along her leg.

A woman in a bright-blue parka approached, the hood ringed with brown-and-black fur trim. At first Kyle thought she might be the checkpoint master coming to check in Kyle and confirm a dog count, but she wasn't carrying a clipboard.

He dropped Ria's paw and stood.

"Whaddya say we take a look at those beautiful dogs of yours," the woman said.

Kyle noticed a rectangular name tag and description pinned just below her shoulder. *Donna Gherna, Head Veterinarian.*

"I was told Jenna would be at this checkpoint," Kyle said.

"Jenna Maynor?" the woman asked.

Kyle realized he didn't actually know Jenna's last name. He thought back to their conversation, but he'd never asked her. It just hadn't seemed pertinent. All he could think to say was, "Red hair?"

The woman smiled, forming wrinkles around her eyes and lips, uncovering her age. "That would be Jenna."

"I hate to be rude, but is there any way I could get her to take a look my dogs?"

"Unfortunately not, but I promise they'll be fine with me."

Kyle shifted his weight onto his left foot and kicked at a frozen pinecone with his right. "I thought she was supposed to be at Braeburn."

"She was, but there was an issue with a couple teams at the starting chute. Several dogs got tangled in the rigging, and she ended up staying behind with them." Donna smiled at Kyle again. "Don't worry. She's supposed to be at Central. I'm sure you'll see here there."

Kyle swung around when he heard a human yelp. About twenty yards to his left, a cameraman nearly tripped over one of Ewan's dog. It was Huey, the curly-haired kid from before. He still clung to the same notepad, while his camera dangled from his neck.

Ewan grabbed him by collar of his coat and pulled him to the side of his team. "Are you dense?"

Huey didn't look much older than Kyle, and before Huey could shake his head, Ewan screamed at him again. "There's fourteen dogs here, tied to a sled, stretched out over fifty feet!"

Kyle took several steps toward the two, until the woman tapped Kyle on the shoulder.

"Come on," she said. "We can take a look at them together."

41

Kyle exhaled a cloud of warm breath as the checkpoint manager coaxed Ewan into letting go of Huey.

"All right," he said.

The woman held out her hand, "I'm Donna, by the way."

Kyle took her gloved hand in his. The silicone tips of his fleece gloves scrunched against hers. "I'm Kyle."

"Yes, we all know you very well, Mr. Walker."

Kyle wasn't sure if that was meant as an insult or praise. Part of him wanted to defend himself, but he didn't want to waste the energy.

Donna knelt by King first, and Kyle tensed. King wasn't unfriendly, just defensive sometimes, especially around new people. Especially when it involved new people poking and prodding at his pack.

She held out her hand, and King slowly bent toward it, his nose wiggling as he inhaled her scent. Was she friend or foe?

He stood, reticent, and licked a piece of ice clinging to her glove. Donna took the glove off and laid it on the ground in front of King, and again he licked her hand, but this time it was the warm flesh of her palm.

Kyle tried to relax, knowing the other dogs would look to him first for the right reaction. So he squatted down next to Donna and clasped his arms across his legs.

"So this is your leader?" she said.

Kyle nodded.

"I've never seen a Carolina gray before." She gazed at King, moving her hand slowly across the coarse hairs that lined his cheek, and finding the soft fur behind his ears and down his crest. "The way he holds his frame, the scene in his eyes, it's almost like he's…"

"Searching," Kyle said.

Donna glanced over at Kyle. "Searching for what?"

"The truth," Kyle said. "Your truth."

For a moment Donna didn't move, and neither did King. She knelt and King sat, both in the scattered hay…searching. King's lips parted, and his tongue fell from his mouth in several pants and then slobbered Donna's face.

"Okay, mister," Donna said. "The tongue looks good, but let me see those feet of yours." She turned to Kyle. "I almost forgot. Do you have your vet book?"

Kyle tromped back to his sled, unzipped a small pocket near the handlebar, and pulled out a bright-yellow book with the words *Dog Team Diary* printed on the front.

"Here you go," he said.

"Thank you much." Donna stood and flipped open the book and filled out the checkpoint name, musher name, vet name, and put a check mark by *comprehensive exam*. Another systematic examination protocol to get used to.

While Kyle had no official training as a vet, his uncle, Doc, had been a military doctor and worked with equine and large animals on a regular basis back home. So when Donna checked the gums to make sure the mucous membrane color was pink and the capillary refill time was less than one second, he knew exactly what she was doing.

She spent about five minutes with each dog, also examining their heart and respiratory rates. Her hands moved over each dog's shoulder, carpal, hip, stifle joint, and tarsal, checking for flexion and general appearance. She asked Kyle questions about each dog. "Any coughing, diarrhea, gait changes?"

Everything was fine until she got to Ria. Kyle had coated her and blanketed her, but she was still shaking.

Donna removed the stethoscope from Ria. "Pulse is a little high."

"How high is it?" Kyle said.

"It's not that high, about one hundred fifteen," she said. "But the shivering is bothering me, especially with a coat, blanket, and hay."

Kyle stepped in front of Ria, who was curled up next to Artemis. The last thing he wanted was to drop a dog. He'd been through two races without a single drop, and he wasn't about to start now.

He pulled the blanket off her and unzipped her coat.

"I don't think that's a good idea," Donna said. "I'm worried she's struggling to keep the heat in."

Kyle ignored Donna and ran his hand across Ria's back and leaned forward until his chest was pressed against her back. Her body was warm. He pressed his fingers against her ears, feeling the warm and waxy skin. *She's not cold. It's something else.*

Kyle pushed away from her, still kneeling next to her. His eyes scanned her trembling body. *She's not cold...*

He leaned back against her, sinking his face into her black fur. His right hand rested on her back, while his left covered her eyes. He breathed with her as she breathed. *In, out, in, out, in, out.* Kyle said her name with the same cadence of her inhale and exhale. "Riiiaaa, Riiiaaa, Riiiaaa."

The trembling stopped. Kyle removed his hand from her eyes. "Calm, girl. We will be back on the trail soon."

Donna looked at Kyle like she had seen a ghost.

"She's not cold," he said. "She's just anxious."

With that, he left Donna still kneeling in the snow and walked toward the Braeburn Lodge. He was craving one of those giant cinnamon rolls.

8

TWO PHOTOGRAPHERS followed Ken Ellis out of Braeburn Lodge. He looked tired already, his wire-rim glasses held up by dark pockets under his eyes. He left Whitehorse in position two, which would have given him at least thirty minutes on Kyle, but he must have run his dogs hard to be leaving the first checkpoint so soon.

Kyle picked up a cinnamon roll from kitchen counter and paid the young girl behind the cash register. He noticed a purple scrunchy holding back her ponytail and wondered what Jenna would look like with her hair pulled back.

There were several empty tables along the wall, but he chose the one farthest from the door. Plastic green laminate covered the seats, and air whooshed out of the foam rubber when he sat down.

Several beads of warm cream cheese oozed down the side of the golden-brown dough, and his eyes traced the cinnamon that spun around in three perfect circles.

Six years ago he was a thirteen-year-old boy training the rarest dog breed in the world with nothing but a stick and some rope. Six months ago he was struggling to sleep in the barn loft back in South Carolina, waiting for this day to come. Six days ago he was poring over old maps, books, and interviews, still taking in everything he could about the Yukon Quest. And here he sat at the first checkpoint, a warm cinnamon roll in front of him, his dogs resting just outside, ready to take on anything he asked them to. One day of the Quest completed, and he didn't feel any more accomplished. It made him wonder, *What's the point of all of this?*

The answer to that question would have to wait because Huey, uninvited, sat down across from him.

"What's a Carolina gray?" Huey said. He set a small handheld recorder on the table and folded back a sheet of his notebook.

Kyle stared at the young reporter. One ear hung lower than the other, and his nose was crooked, like maybe he'd broken it when he was younger and it hadn't healed right.

"Oh, sorry. I'm Huey. Some of the guys call me Baby Huey because I guess I look younger, but I'm not actually that young. Been doing this for three years now. I work for *Sled Dog Daily*. Actually, it's SledDogDaily.com—it's my blog. But *Fairbanks Daily* is contracting me. So I'm really writing for them. It's not my first race, if that's what you're thinking. I'm..."

Apparently Huey's altercation with Ewan did little to intimidate him, because he didn't stop talking. Kyle finally put both of his hands up, and Huey went silent.

"Fairbanks," Kyle said.

"What?" Huey said. "Fairbanks? That's where the race ends. Did you know they still mine gold just north of there? Several million ounces of gold has been pulled out of there in the last five years alone!"

Kyle rubbed his forehead. "No, I'm not answering any questions until Fairbanks."

"Oh, umm, okay. All right. Well, yeah..."

"I'm going to eat my cinnamon roll now," Kyle said.

"Yeah, yeah, totally. They're delicious. Did you know..."

"Alone," Kyle said.

"Oh, right. Sorry. Okay, I will see you in Fairbanks. Or Dawson or Central. I'll be there too. Oh, and Eagle." Huey grabbed his recorder and notepad and walked over to an empty table.

A few minutes later Kyle wiped away the last drops of cream cheese icing from the corners of his mouth. He probably should have opted for the lasagna that was still frozen in his checkpoint drop bag, but the smell of a fresh-baked cinnamon bun had been too much. Besides, he had another three hours of mandatory layover time.

He tossed his plate in the trash can and walked over to a chair where his socks and anorak were hanging. Kyle lifted the suspenders off his shoulders and stepped out of his trans-Alaskan Gore-Tex bib. He laid them across the chair and scanned the room. No one seemed to care that he was standing there barefoot in nothing but a skintight pair of thermals.

He pushed the chair against the wall and lay down on the vinyl floor. The mandatory rest was too short to bother with a sleeping bag, so Kyle just bunched the hood below his head directly underneath the chair. The last thing he wanted was to be stepped on in the middle of the night. His pants and coat combined with the chair to provide a little shade in the building that would stay lit throughout the night, for other mushers arriving. The watch on his chest said 2131 in military time. He didn't bother to set an alarm though. As awake as he was, sleeping for a couple hours would be hard enough.

Kyle watched the dogs run through the dim light of his headlamp. They knifed through the icy night without a care in the world. But something bothered him as he drove the team though. He studied his gloved hands wrapped around the handlebar. They felt numb against the coarse knots of tape he had wrapped around them two days ago. He tried to squeeze his hands, but he couldn't feel the flex. Even worse, as the sled skated over the snow, he realized he couldn't remember how they got here. How far from Carmacks were they? How many miles had they traveled?

This wasn't an entirely uncommon feeling. On long stretches, especially during the middle of the night, it was easy to lose yourself among the darkness, among the silence. Some mushers used radios or music with headphones to keep them awake, but Kyle normally preferred the stillness.

His mind wandered as he thought back to the last thing he could remember: sleeping at Braeburn.

The yellow light from his headlamp flickered over the team and across the endless expanse. King skirted the team around several scrub willows and over an indistinct down-trail covered in patches of ice. Kyle was thankful for the dogs' ability to adapt to low-light vision, a topic he'd read multiple articles about: a larger pupil to let in more light, and more light-sensitive cells in the center of the retina that worked better in low-light environments.

Still, he couldn't shake this disoriented feeling.

Behind him Kyle could hear another team approach. The dogs called out in a clamor of barks and cries. He could also see a light bounce off the snow around him, but it wasn't his light. It was faint, probably a handheld spotlight from the musher behind him. He lifted one hand off the sled so he could look back, but he saw nothing. No light, no team, just a blinding darkness.

Several minutes later he heard the howls again, but this time the sound was beside him. Up on a ridge about fifty yards to his right, something moved furiously through the woods. It wasn't another musher. It wasn't another team of dogs. The objects maneuvered down the moraine, closing in on his team. The moonlight shimmered across their eyes. A pack of wolves.

Kyle tried to call out. *Hike, King! Hike!* But his throat was frozen solid from the midnight air. Nothing but a frantic breath escaped his lips.

Without warning, one of the wolves tore through the trail's edge and lunged at King—a mistake, even with King tied to the sled and held back by his harness. King sprang forward, and the sled jerked. The wolf's lean legs tangled in the rigging, and Story and Link leapt at the wolf, teeth bared. The wolf was trampled, but it led to the worst possible scenario: the sled rattled to a stop.

Two more wolves descended upon the team. King tried to whip his body around, but the tangled wolf anchored his harness to the ground.

Kyle staggered off the runners and toward his dogs. He reached down to the boot where a knife was strapped and then sliced down on the jumbled lines. A fourth wolf surged, but Kyle could do nothing as the massive beast leapt at him.

The wolf's force knocked Kyle to the ground, and the animal's powerful paws on his chest pressed him deeper into the snow. Its frothing mouth glittered in the effulgent energy of their moonlit surroundings.

King let loose a bloodcurdling scream that sounded more human than dog.

"Kiiiiingggg!" Kyle screamed out. "Kiiiingggg!"

A voice in the distance responded. "Kyle. Kyle."

The wolf latched on to Kyle's jacket, and the beast shook his head, ripping the anorak from Kyle's body.

The voice resounded again, this time closer. "Kyle. Kyle."

Kyle jolted up, banging his head on the chair he had been sleeping under, and sent it clanging to the floor.

Donna stood over him. "Kyle, are you okay?"

He surveyed the room. Two mushers looked at him strangely, their heads cocked. *It's all just a dream. Just a dream.*

* * *

Milkshake must have made it to the checkpoint sometime while Kyle slept, because the bulky man's booming voice carried throughout the room as he got dressed. He sat at a high-top table in the center of the room, his massive body spilling over the barstool.

"I had a fan once tell me that more people had climbed Mount Everest than completed the Iditarod," Milkshake said.

"I've read that before," a shaggy-haired reporter said.

"Yeah," agreed another reporter.

"But you know what I said to him? I said, 'Yup, and even less have completed the Yukon Quest.'" Milkshake slapped his tree-like knee and winked at the guy.

Kyle, resting on his elbows, viewed the shaggy-haired journalist jot something down.

Ryne Moore and Frank Lesh were no longer at the lodge, and neither was Huey. A musher he didn't recognize occupied the corner of the room where Ewan had been sitting; Ewan was gone.

Kyle scooted out from under the chair and looked at his watch: 0003. It was officially day two of the Yukon Quest, and even though it was the middle of the night with temperatures dipping around negative ten degrees Fahrenheit, it was time to go to work.

King sprang to his feet as Kyle approached, letting loose a ringing howl. Ria and Story joined in, while their counterparts, Link and Artemis, stretched out their forelegs, bending at the hips in each direction. Giza, Hali, and Sunshine barked when another team ambled into the checkpoint, while Colossus and Olympia both sniffed at the myriad of smells escaping the lodge.

Kyle looked at his wheel dogs. "You just had a half pound of chicken, beef fat, and kibble, and you're still hungry?"

Colossus lips parted, and his tongue lapped across his nose. He started to pant lightly, like a fat old man smiling.

"We'll get you another snack in a few hours. Sound good?" Colossus and Olympia barked at Kyle.

Kyle didn't doubt the dogs were sated after consuming upward of ten thousand calories, but they'd need more soon. Therein lay the art of mushing: keeping the dogs healthy, hydrated, and well fed. A good dog would give signs of any malnourishment or problems, but a great musher never let it come to that. And Kyle intended to be the best musher. He was certain Colossus and Olympia were responding to the scents, not to actual hunger pangs.

51

A man carrying a clipboard strode forward. "You heading out?"

"Yes, sir," Kyle said.

"All right, let me get a quick head count. Two, four, six, eight, ten, twelve…thirteen? Ah, single lead. I see the note here. All right, you're good to go."

"When did Ewan leave?" Kyle asked.

The man looked back down at his clipboard. "Right…about…twelve minutes ago."

"Do you know who's leading right now?"

"Sorry. I don't. I do know two teams have stayed longer than the mandatory four hours, and ten teams are ahead of Ewan, and you'll make eleven."

That means Ewan and I have picked up two spots in the first checkpoint. "Okay, thanks."

"Be safe out there!"

Kyle nodded.

He walked through his typical routine of checking the towline where it attached to the sled, and each of the tug lines and neck lines attached to the dog harnesses and collars. He unclipped Story and flaked out a few twists in the line, then clipped her back in and stepped behind the sled.

"Line out, King."

King marched forward several steps until the line was tight between him and the sled. Story lunged forward, jerking the sled about an inch. Ria did the same. They were ready.

"Hike!" Kyle yelled. "Hike, hike, hike!"

The sled glided into motion like a locomotive leaving the station. First slowly, overcoming the friction of the runners in the trace, until the dogs found their stride and broke into a full run. The dogs seemed to relish the cold temperatures of a

Yukon night and propelled forward around fifteen miles per hour. Kyle's Carolina grays weren't the workhorses of a typical Alaskan husky, but they were faster. They were smarter. And they would catch Ewan.

9

AFTER A FEW HOURS Kyle found himself in an all-too-familiar darkness. His headlamp swept a shadowy light over the team, and his gaze flicked up to the listless ridges on their right, and then behind him. Nothing. He tried not to keep looking, but his mind played tricks on him. He glanced again. No other musher, no wolves. Just the stillness. Just the deep, dark, distance.

Over the next one hundred and fifty miles, Kyle fought through the fog of his mind and the radiating fog that camped around them and clung to the trees like cotton on a cold day. The trail was downhill through Braeburn and Pelly Crossing, with the ever-looming King Solomon's Dome jutting up over four thousand feet through the lowland mist in front of them.

A bit of drift snow powdered the trail, but Kyle was glad for once to be behind Ewan and several others who broke the path for him and his dogs.

The other teams' exhaustion was clear when Kyle passed several snacking and sleeping on the side of the trail. It was about an hour into day four, and by his count there were still six teams in front of him with a long way to go.

A few hours later the dogs handled King Solomon's Dome with ease as the sun rose in front of them. After a few hours of rest, the team cruised over American Summit later that night, even with winds whipping around forty miles per hour and temperatures dropping past negative thirty. Kyle's arms shook from holding the brake bar up, and he was worried about the dogs moving so fast down the backside of American Summit, but at this pace they were most efficient. His biceps ached, and his eyes burned from the ice glare doubling the sun back at him. It was slippery, and the dogs scuttled across with shorter steps, but not once did they falter.

Midmorning on the sixth day, Eagle checkpoint came into view as the downslope of American flattened. Kyle let go of the brake, and the dogs eased up relative to the decreased resistance.

"Goo ggrr Olymiuh. Goo bo Colossuh." The frozen wind stole his words and burned his throat. He bent his head forward into the fur lining of his collar and used it as a filter to breathe in and out warm air and thaw his mouth and throat.

"Keep it up, Hali and Sunshine! Straight on, King! Straight on!"

The dogs ran well, their backs flat, their gaits smooth. It wasn't until a few hundred yards shy of Eagle checkpoint, just over the halfway point of the thousand-mile race, that he ran into a problem: Ria was limping.

* * *

With a mandatory six-hour layover at Eagle, Kyle spent nearly every minute rubbing the triceps, shoulders, and feet of the dogs. He wrapped Ria's leg in a tight neoprene brace to help keep in the heat, but there was no way she was running out of this checkpoint. There was also no way he was dropping her.

Several people were standing around a split-log fire, taking pictures and chatting. Kyle walked past them to the drop sack with his name on it. He dug through it until he found a square Tupperware container with frozen spaghetti.

The green door to Eagle Public School swung open, and Ryne Moore walked out. He nodded at Kyle and pushed it open enough for Kyle to slip in. The old schoolhouse was a single-room building that had been preserved mostly as a landmark.

A half-dozen folding tables and plastic chairs were scattered throughout the room, and along the wall to his right, a musher was sprawled facedown on his sleeping bag. Kyle remembered his name was Tom, but spelled differently, like Thom, or Tomh. He was Norwegian.

There was a table along the opposite wall, with two coffeepots, a microwave, a toaster, and a few cups of plastic silverware, which was good, because his container of spaghetti didn't have its normal spork taped to the outside.

After a few minutes of nuking the pasta and meat sauce, Kyle found a table near the door, where one of the volunteers was seated. Two bites in, and someone sat down next to him.

Without looking up from his meal, Kyle immediately recognized the quick-paced voice of Huey.

"Is she going to be your first drop?"

Kyle heard the hushed words from a few others a couple tables away. One of the reporters he usually saw with Ewan scribbled something on a piece of paper and then joined Kyle, Huey, and the volunteer, who was busy picking his fingernails with a knife.

"Mr. Walker, right?" the new reporter said. He held out his hand across the table from Kyle. "My name is Joe Wright. I work for ESPN."

Kyle finished another bite and shook the man's hand.

Joe licked his finger and flipped several pages on his notepad. "This is your first Yukon Quest, right?"

Kyle nodded, but he was focused on chewing each bite of his food. He was starving, but the last thing he wanted to do was inhale a bunch of spaghetti and end up with a stomachache somewhere between here and Circle City.

"You're in fourth place right now. Still a lot of race left, but—and don't take this the wrong way—you're one of the mushers we didn't expect to be on the heels of people like Frank Lesh, two-time Quest champion and Iditarod champion; and Ryne Moore, three-time Iditarod champion; and Ewan Harbinson, three-time and reigning Quest champion."

You're in fourth. Kyle repeated the words in his head. He had been pushing the dogs longer and longer between breaks. They'd run well, but they hadn't hit their stride. *You're in fourth,* he repeated again. Kyle set his fork down and looked up at the man sitting across from him.

"Was that a question?"

"Well, how do you feel about that?" Joe said.

"I'm tired and I'm hungry," Kyle said.

"But how do you feel about being in the top five this late in the race? I hope you don't mind me asking, but do you think you have what it takes to keep this up?"

"No," Kyle said.

"No?" Joe said. "Because you've got to drop a couple dogs?"

"No, not dropping any dogs," Kyle said.

"And what do you attribute the health of your dogs to?"

"Luck," Kyle said.

"That's it?" Joe said. "No secret training tips?"

Kyle picked at a piece of oregano stuck between his teeth. "Dogs are a lot like people, Mr. Wright. Keep 'em clean. Keep 'em eating well. Get 'em some rest. Let the vets do their job, and that's about all you can do."

He finished off his spaghetti but still thought about Joe's first question. He didn't like answering questions, but tossing out some breadcrumbs every now and then kept the reporters full. He tossed his container in the trash can behind him and stood up to face Joe, still sitting, pencil pressed to the page.

"I don't think much about the top five, and I don't plan on keeping this pace."

"Because you'll have to drop some dogs?" Joe asked again.

"I'm not dropping any dogs, Mr. Wright," Kyle said again.

Huey had been strangely quiet this entire time, and he followed Kyle outside with a huge grin on his face.

Huey held his finger to his lips. "Thank you, Mr. Walker. It'll be our little secret."

"I honestly have no idea what you're talking about," Kyle said.

"The dogs," Huey said. "They don't know."

"They don't know what?" Kyle said.

Huey leaned in and whispered. "That...that they're Carolina grays."

"What do you mean, *they* don't know?"

"Well, I mean the vets know. Because they gotta pay attention to that stuff. Some of the mushers know, because they know dogs. But the other reporters—they don't know." Huey went on. "They don't know about the two-year-old that runs in front of your wheel dogs. The way she moves like water, both smooth like an ocean and swift like a river. Or the three-year-old that runs behind your leader and moves with the

58

effervescent energy of the sun." Huey looked around the room and then back at Kyle. "They don't know about King. I've seen dogs run, Mr. Walker. And I ain't ever seen anything like them. It's subtle, like the touch of a feather on a windy day. But it's there."

* * *

Kyle woke up to the incessant chirp of his watch alarm. For a moment he was back in Bishopville. The dogs needed to be fed, he needed to go for a run, and then after some training, he could finish sketching out his idea for some new kennels, assuming Doc approved of it.

The smell of fresh coffee filled the room, along with the constant flood of artificial lights backdropped by the coming night. He sat up in his sleeping bag and snapped back into the present moment.

It was nearly two days to the next checkpoint, Circle City. Another day to Central. And about a half day each to Mile 101, Two Rivers, and finally Fairbanks. With less than five days left, Kyle unloaded items from his sled that he could drop at Eagle: a bit of straw, an extra parka, a fleece blanket, and some miscellaneous rigging. He had to make room for two dogs. Artemis would be fine to run unpaired, but he knew the old dog could use a little rest. And it would drive Ria insane to view her mate from the sled instead of being beside him on the trail.

Just as he settled the dogs in the sled and lined out, two vets ran past him, followed by several volunteers clad in reflective vests and carrying flashlights. Justin Beal, the only other musher under twenty, pulled his team to a stop. He threw out a snow hook and knelt by his sled.

One of the vets yelled at a volunteer who wouldn't move out of the way. Kyle's dogs started barking and baying with the other team. It was hard to see what happened, but the dog on Justin's sled wasn't moving.

The scolded volunteer walked past Kyle, muttering something under his breath.

"What happened?" Kyle asked.

The guy turned around. "Huh?"

Kyle pointed over to Justin's sled and the crowd that was gathering. "What happened?"

"Oh, I don't know. Musher got tired at night. Veered the dogs off course because he thought he saw something. One of them got tripped up on a soft spot in the ice. Looks like the front two legs are broken. Not sure."

The man started to walk away, but Kyle asked him another question. "What did he see?"

"Huh?"

"You said he thought he saw something."

"Oh yeah, he thought he saw a moose on the trail."

Kyle pulled out of Eagle in fourth, just a few hours behind Ewan and two others. Circle City was 160 miles away, and he'd need to camp at least one night, but Kyle had his eyes set on Central, where he knew Jenna would be.

10

THE STRETCH between Eagle and Central was wide open and subject to winds of more than eighty miles an hour. The trail had been easygoing while the sun still shone. But as the oranges and yellows seeped from behind a sky framed with endless ridges, twilight approached, and with it the wind.

At first it was no more than a steady breeze from the north. Kyle ignored it, along with the dark, by singing every song he could remember. He settled on "Breathe" by Faith Hill, and eventually just two words from the song: *just breathe*. He sang it over and over to the dogs. Ria joined in from the sled, as did Spirit, Shyanne, and Story. It was a cacophony of sounds that the wind carried to places Kyle would never even see, and they serenaded the wilds together for hours.

Their song was interrupted when the team rode upon a fallen tree jutting into the trail.

"Haw, haw!" Kyle yelled. Story and Link pulled to their left, then King, then the rest of the team. They passed the tree, and Kyle ushered another command to direct them back on the trail. "Gee, gee!" The sled quickly veered back to the right and into the ruts of the sleds that had passed in front of them.

"Good dogs!" Kyle said. "Great job, Story. Good job, Link. Keep it up, King." Spirit and Shyanne let loose several short yips. "You too, girls. Good job!" They bayed into the tide of the night.

"Just think," Kyle said. "We could all be back at home right now, instead of busting our butts our here. Not on the outskirts of Whitehorse, where we spent the last six months, but in Bishopville. Hanging out in the barn together, watching shadows dance on the walls from the flickering oil lamps, just talking about life."

King stirred, and his throaty growl transformed into a reverberating howl. The pitch echoed throughout the land, and several of the dogs joined in. A few seconds later, another team responded, tracking somewhere in front of Kyle.

"What else is on your mind tonight, King?"

King's sable coat shone in the starlight. He let out a short series of noises that were somewhere between a bark and howl. "Roo, roooh, roooo!"

"Oh really? You want to know what's on my mind? I know I should be focused on the race, but I can't help but think about her."

Artemis looked back at him. In the night, Kyle couldn't see the black-and-brown pools of Artemis' eyes, but the light-tan markings above them moved.

"Don't give me that look," Kyle said. "You know who I'm talking about."

Curled up next to Artemis in the sled, Ria flicked her gaze back to Kyle too. "No, I don't like her more than you. Geez. I just...I don't know. You know when someone's just got that something about them? It just pulls you in."

Kyle looked up at the crescent moon, no bigger than a sliver of silver in the sky. "She's pretty too. Not just the way she looks, but the way she moves, like...like water."

Ria sat up completely and joined Artemis, both of whom were now staring directly at him. "I told you, I don't like her more than you. But I can't help it. You know we held hands? Her hands were cold, but it felt like warm water when she touched me. You know? Like when you wake up on a January morning and run out of the barn into the sunny grass and just stretch and roll and play. That's what it felt like."

Ria moaned.

"What? No, I've held hands with a girl before."

Ria tilted her head to the side and stared at Kyle.

"Okay, fine, I haven't, but I've been busy with you guys. Someone has to spend half the week picking up your poop."

Artemis barked.

"Oh, don't even. Doc barely does anything! Yeah, sure, he does all his fancy doctor stuff, but come on. I'm the one who feeds you, rakes up all that dirty straw, fills your water pails—and by the way, I don't know how y'all don't just pee all day long."

Kyle thought about Doc and wondered what he'd be doing right now. It was nearly two in the morning in Alaska, which meant it was six in the morning in South Carolina. Doc had probably been up for an hour or more. *He's probably on his second cup of coffee. The other dogs would be up by now too. Raley and Raggles, Boone and Wyatt. Dixie, Jade, Biscuit, Belle...*

He missed them all.

Kyle flexed his hands inside a combination of beaver fur, wool, and hand warmers. The tips of his fingers tingled either from the blood rushing throughout his hands as they tightened around the bow, or because he'd damaged some of the nerves in this extreme cold.

63

After passing Slaven's Roadhouse, several other shelter cabins sprouted up on the outskirts of the trail. Kyle brushed away chips of ice frozen to his unshaven face. He could still barely feel his hands, and couldn't tell if his feet were even touching the running boards. The team was moving slower, and they still had over a hundred miles until Central.

He searched his mind for more stories or thoughts he could share with the dogs, but all he found was a void. A blankness. Not like a cave of bad things. Just…emptiness. Just nothing. To each side of him the scattered cabins started to blend in with fields of jumble ice the size of cars and as hard as mountains. He needed to stop.

"Easy, King. Easy." After a few seconds the sled coasted to a standstill. Kyle pinched the button on his headlamp, and thin yellow light washed over the ground. Just in front of King, about five feet off the trail, was a mixture of packed ice and snow. It wouldn't be comfortable, but it was sheltered by a massive chunk of ice that looked like a hobbit hole.

He eased the team into the mild break and started to spread the last of the straw. The dogs shook loose bits of dirty brown snow and chunks of ice from their faces and coats before lying down. Spirit slid her face against the snow, scratching an itch.

Kyle broke off several branches of a beetle-eaten spruce and dropped them in a pile in the center of the dogs. He stamped out a flat spot and built a platform out of several pieces of timber, just high enough to sit above the snow line. He patted his hands over his jacket pockets for the three things that never left his side: a serrated-blade knife, a bag of Vaseline-drenched cotton balls, and waterproof matches.

He pulled out one of the cotton balls from the plastic baggy in his pocket and lit it atop the platform, beneath a tepee-like structure of spruce. Within minutes he had his bunny boots and socks drying by the fire and his feet propped up just inches from the growing flames. King walked over and plopped down next to Kyle as he tried to wring the cold out of his feet and toes with his bare hands.

Their circle of light glowed alone in the midst of the white plains. Kyle stared into the flames, and they stared back like a moving soul.

Sunshine nipped and licked at her toes, where ice had recently collected, and Hali curled up beside her in a snug ball.

Kyle rubbed the matted and wet fur along King's nape and down his crest. "How you doin', buddy?"

King squeaked out a yawn.

"Yeah, me too." Kyle said. "Me too."

In ideal conditions Kyle would have searched out some rocks to cook in the fire in order to make a warm bed of coals below him. But the wind walked between the ravines of ice like people scurrying through a big city on Monday morning. So instead, he unrolled his sleeping bag and pulled himself inside. King curled up next to his face, and Story by his feet. Little flakes of fur blew over him, and he sneezed twice.

Kyle had disconnected the sled from the gangline so he could position it on the other side of him, where Ria and Artemis remained. He rolled his head to the left and watched Ria bury her face into the rugged Codura fabric that lined the sled bag.

"You all comfy now, girl?" Kyle said.

Ria let out a puff of breath from her nose, and Artemis did the same.

"I'm tired too," Kyle said. "I'm tired too."

He closed his eyes and spoke to Ria and Artemis again. "Give those legs a good rest tonight, and we'll see about getting you off the sled tomorrow."

A grunting noise came from near Kyle's feet. "Mmmhmpf."

It was Story. Bedtime was bedtime, not talk time. She moaned again. "Uhmmmmpfh."

"All right, all right," Kyle. "Good night, everyone."

Wild sounds surrounding Kyle grew louder as his team faded off to sleep. The incessant hoot of a Northern saw-whet owl echoed over the Yukon like a child blowing incessantly on a kazoo, along with the occasional saw-like chirp of a katydid that had survived the winter.

Kyle repeated the trail report in his head as he lay there. *Usual mix of deep snow, ice, rock, gravel, and wind-blown silt. Hard rain crust on snow forty-five miles out of Eagle. Some jumble ice, past mile fifty, but hardly any past Slaven's Cabin. Open leads near mile seventy and ninety. Trout Creek, Kandik, and Brian's Cabin are currently open.* Kyle had never ran the trail from Eagle to Central, but he knew what lay ahead.

11

MORNING LIGHT swooped down like an eagle after prey and spread across Kyle and the dogs. The dogs were alert, even as they lay there resting. Ears twitching and pivoting, nostrils quivering.

The entire atmosphere was different at daybreak. The wind was gone, and the sun filled every particle of air with jubilant energy. Kyle worked better in a little warmth, but knew the fastest path to Central would be one with the dogs running in temperatures below zero—in other words, at night.

An ashen ring was all that was left of the fire, but Kyle no longer needed it. All mushers carried methanol and a specialized cooker large enough to heat at least three gallons of water. He pulled out several packs of vacuum-sealed meals from the sled bag below Ria, and let them defrost in the boiling water.

He unfolded his knife and slit open the top of the bags once they were thawed, mixing a bit of water with chunks of chicken, kibble, and vitamins.

They sopped up the stew of chicken and kibble from their stainless steel bowls as Kyle walked among them. He straightened their jackets and harnesses. He massaged their legs and quickly inspected their feet. He checked their eyes and ears, and the nooks around them, for any signs of frostbite or gooseflesh.

Lastly, Kyle inspected Ria. He spent more time with her than the others, applying a warm wrapping of neoprene on her forelegs. She walked over the trail, testing them out while Kyle watched. Her steps were more sure, more solid, but he couldn't risk it. Another day on the sled, and they'd be in Central. He'd need her and Artemis at full strength for the last few legs of the race.

"Sorry, girl," he said. "It's back in the basket for you today."

Kyle cleaned the area where they had slept, and he clipped the dogs back in to the tug lines. The watch that hung from the handlebar read 0641 in boxed black numbers backlit in indigo. He was worried they had rested too long, that maybe they wouldn't catch the three mushers in front of them, or even worse, had been passed in the night by others. But when he pulled the hook, all worries disappeared.

"Hike, King!"

Colossus and Olympia were sluggish to start as the sled creaked into motion. "Let's go, Colossus! Come on, Olympia!" Kyle shouted the words in short bursts. "Hike, hike, hike!"

What was initially a slow start turned into one of the best paces Kyle had hit throughout the race. The ground was littered with a couple inches of last night's snow. Any more snow would have forced the dogs to break trail, but this amount had a pliable give that softened their steps.

In the daylight the jumble ice appeared even more daunting as the team zigzagged past cabin-sized boulders roofed with packed snow nailed together by nature itself. The sled bumped, bounced, and banged around the trail. It was hard going for

Kyle, as the reverberations from the aluminum runners and white ash stanchions sent jolts through his lower body.

King swerved around a loose chunk of accumulated graupel. Link looked out to the right at the endless white megadunes, but he instinctively leapt over the bricked ice at the last minute.

"Good boy, Link!" Kyle said as the sled swerved to the left. "Gee, gee!" The sled moved back into the trace, and Kyle scanned the oncoming trail. He was always looking one foot and one mile ahead. He wanted to know two things: what was directly in front of them, and what nature was hiding in the horizon.

It would be too overwhelming to look at the trail as a whole. Traveling one thousand miles was more than any mind could truly appreciate. So Kyle broke down the thousand-mile journey into days, and the days into runs. Each run was four, six, and sometimes eight hours of endless burn. The million billion synapses in his brain to the hundreds of sinews in his body burned. And as the team skirted the edges of the Klondike Loop and Kyle watched in awe as they passed under the Icefield Ranges of the Saint Elias Mountains, notorious for some of the coldest temperatures recorded, one truth about this incessant burn screamed louder than any other: no matter how bad it hurt, it could always hurt worse, but together, they could always endure more.

Overhead, Kyle heard the electric whirl of a helicopter.

* * *

Several thousand feet overhead, Joe had a bird's-eye view of the race from a cockpit of an old Bell news copter that ESPN had rented out. The KUAC TV9—a local Fairbanks affiliate of

PBS—helicopter hovered above several teams trekking through the open pass to Central checkpoint.

"Isn't this just beautiful up here?" said Mike, the pilot, as he held the cyclic stick steady. This was Mike's fifth straight year flying during the Yukon Quest—but it was Joe's first.

Joe looked through a pair of binoculars at two teams making their way between Circle City and Central. "It is incredible," Joe said. He flicked the stopwatch that he was holding and tapped Mike on the shoulder. "This can't be right."

"Everything okay up there, guys?" Stanton said from a live radio broadcast room in Fairbanks.

"Oh yeah," Joe said. He spoke into the gray aviation headset. "Forgot we were live for a minute there. Right now we're watching Kyle Walker's team about seventy miles outside of Central."

"So what can't be right?" Stanton asked.

"Well, Mike and I have been checking each team's speed. The surveyor laths below are about five hundred feet apart. So I can measure the time it takes the team to pass two stakes and convert that into a speed."

"Right, right," Stanton said. "Pretty standard. I think you said Ryne Moore was about five miles ahead of Kyle Walker, moving around eleven or twelve miles per hour."

"Yep, we checked it several times. That's right," Joe said.

"So how is Mr. Walker's team doing? We weren't really expecting a rookie musher to be in the top four this late in the race. I'm assuming his team is starting to slow down a bit as they approach the last few checkpoints?"

Joe punched the stopwatch with his thumb and scribbled down the numbers. The math was right, and he'd checked it four times now. "Well, ummm, let's put it this way. Kyle Walker will catch Ryne's team within the hour at this rate."

"He's moving at sixteen miles per hour?" Stanton asked.

"No," Joe said.

"But I thought you said he'd catch him within—"

Joe cut him off. "He's moving close to twenty."

"Wait," Stanton said. "Twenty miles per hour?"

Mike hovered the copter over the trail and looked over at Joe in disbelief. *Twenty miles per hour?* he mouthed.

"That's not even the best part," Joe said. "He's got two dogs in the basket."

"So twenty miles per hour with twelve dogs on the ground?"

"Eleven," Joe said. "He's running single lead with this massive beast of a dog driving them. I've never seen this before."

"That's right," Stanton said. "I guess I'm still a little shocked he went out single lead."

"They're running uphill too," Mike said.

Joe held his hand over the receiver. "What?"

"Yeah, from Circle City to Central is a plus-three-hundred-foot elevation change."

The radio went silent for a moment. "I…I don't know what to say," Stanton said.

"Well," Joe said. "Jack London once said that achieving greatness sometimes means burning white hot, even if there's a price to be paid once the flame goes out. I'm afraid he'll be paying that price at the next checkpoint if he tries to maintain this pace."

"Well, ladies and gentleman of the great Yukon, we've got a rookie musher by the name of Kyle Walker, a name you'll likely be hearing more of, two spots behind defending champion Ewan 'the Hammer' Harbinson, nipping at the heels of veteran Ryne Moore, and racing uphill at nearly twenty miles per hour...with eleven dogs. No, they're not purebred Alaskan huskies or malamutes. He's not running husky-hound mixes with the speed of a German shorthair or English pointer. No, ladies and gentleman, let me introduce you to a dog native to the lowlands of South Carolina."

Joe could hear Stanton riffling through papers.

"Meet the Carolina gray," Stanton said. "Led ferociously by a lead dog named King."

* * *

Four thousand five hundred and seventy miles away, a man in his early sixties with a shabby white beard sat smiling on his porch. He pushed down the silver antenna and turned off his portable AM/FM radio. The wooden rocking chair moaned underneath his massive frame.

Doc reached down next to him and rubbed a certain spot behind Biscuit's ear. "They don't know, do they, Biscuit? They think he's emptying the tank too soon."

Doc stood up and stretched his hands overhead. He grabbed his walking stick that was lying against the front door. "Come on, girl. Let's go tell the others."

Doc stumbled and caught himself against the barn door. He squeezed the painted red timber and coughed several times.

Biscuit barked as she trotted to a stop next to Doc.

"Hold on a minute," Doc said, pulling a handkerchief out of his pocket. He blew his nose and dabbed his mouth. "Give this old man a break, would ya?"

He folded the white lace kerchief and leaned over the stall where Belle sat. His fingers hesitated before sliding it into his pocket, when they found the stitched initials of his late wife embroidered into the fabric.

The young female stood up on her hind legs, wagged her foxlike tail, and peppered Doc's face with wet kisses.

"Good girl," Doc said. "Good girl. Now go tell the others that Kyle's in fourth place."

She barked at the sound of her master's name, and Dixie, Jade, and Maynard joined in.

"Let the world know," Doc said to the dogs. "Kyle Walker is running fourth..." He choked off several tears and held them burning in his throat. One snuck by as he whispered to himself, "That's my boy."

12

KYLE WATCHED as King led the team out of the jumble ice and back onto the Yukon River. This area, along with the Forty-mile stretch, was considered among the coldest on the trail, and Kyle knew temperatures could drop as low as negative sixty or seventy. He was thankful they were close to Central and the sun was shining heavy.

The conditions lasted for a couple hours, but the free-ranging trail, unprotected on both sides, once again unveiled its frosty face. The dogs slowed, and Kyle pinched his hood shut around his face, leaving only enough space to keep the trail in his eyes.

Ryne's team had been in his sight lines for the past ten minutes, but now they were only a couple hundred feet away. The trail cut a wide sluice through the tundra, and Ryne looked back at Kyle several times. Kyle knew he could call trail. The passing team always had the right of way, but Kyle found a strange sense of pride in driving his team past another.

He waited until he heard a familiar, but faint, call from Ryne. "Gee! Gee!" Ryne's dogs moved to the right.

Kyle called out to King. "Straight on, King! Straight on!"

They passed Ryne's team, and Kyle leaned back on the sled rails to try and prevent any extra snow or ice from kicking up into the other team. He looked back between the slit in his hood and collar, and then one foot and one mile ahead.

It was late afternoon by the time Kyle reached Central checkpoint. The dogs' faces were covered in hoarfrost, and places on their coats were matted with ice. Ryne and his team were a few hours behind him and clearly tiring from the freezing wind.

Kyle had been questioned by reporters and journalists at every checkpoint since Whitehorse, but as he pulled into Central, a small band of cameras approached, flashing electric sounds and crowding around his dogs. From this point on, winning came down to only a handful of teams, and the reporters clearly wanted to know more about a rookie musher named Kyle Walker.

The dogs barked at the flashing lights and high-pitched electronic whirring from the cameras. King reared up on his hind legs and bit at the air in front of him as they neared. This had the opposite effect that King wanted, as the cameras moved closer, and he let out a series of short barks.

"All right, all right," a plump-faced man with a clipboard said. "Let the man get settled in."

The reporters ignored the man until he rapped on his clipboard. "Hey! Inside. Let's go. Give Mr. Walker some space. He'll be in after he gets the dogs settled and checked in."

"Sorry about that," he said to Kyle once they were gone. "I'm Jed, by the way."

Kyle shook the man's hand, and the skin below his chin jiggled along with it. "I'm Kyle."

"Yes, sir, everyone's been talking about your run from Eagle to here."

"I don't much like the cameras," Kyle said.

"Yeah, I know that too…"

"Near the dogs," he finished. "At all."

"Understood. I'll pass on the word. For now though, let me get you checked in real quick." The man pointed at each of the dogs with his pen. "I see eleven on foot and two in the basket. Full team." He motioned toward Ria and Artemis. "You planning on dropping these two?"

Kyle looked down at Ria and winked. "No, sir."

The man scratched his head, and a part of his beanie bunched up over his eyebrows. "All right, well, let me get the vet," the man said.

"Is Jenna here?"

The man smiled. "Yes, sir. She is the vet."

Kyle stepped off the sled and dropped a snow hook to anchor them. He walked around to the side of the sled and rubbed his gloved hands down Ria's neck as he watched Jed make his way out of the cold and into Steese's Roadhouse, the mainstay of Central checkpoint. The man disappeared, but Jenna never appeared.

Near the thick timber building, all but one of Ewan's dogs were curled up on plots of straw. It had taken nine days, but Kyle finally caught Ewan. Kyle's euphoria faded when Ewan unclipped one of his dogs.

The animal bucked free of Ewan's grasp. Kyle had been watching the white husky, splashed with bouts of gray and black. The dog was young, adolescent, body and temperament still changing with his age. It made him unpredictable, dangerous, and ultimately unfit for the trail, in Kyle's opinion. Maybe Ewan knew this. Maybe he didn't.

The husky jerked away from Ewan's outstretched arm and covered the gap to Kyle's team in just a few seconds, and whether the dog meant to make friends and play or lash out with aggression, Kyle didn't know. He broke into a run, and just a few feet before King, he kicked out his legs and slid feet first.

The dog leapt over him, obviously confused by Kyle's maneuvers, and pivoted on his hind legs. He was adjacent to Ria and Artemis in the sled, but kept his eyes set on a place near Kyle.

He ripped off his glove and reached for King's tug line. Just as the husky sprang at him, King was loose. Unlike the husky, or any dog for that matter, King was too wise in the way of dogs to be fooled by one. He offered no warning, only a leap like a flash. King had thirty or forty pounds on this dog and went headlong at him. He curled his lips and bared his teeth, but it never came to that. The struggle for dominance was often not a struggle of physicality or strength, but first a struggle of the pure and brilliant energy of the mind—in which King easily bested the younger canine.

The husky went limp in the snow, bowing and ducking his head to a growling King. Story and Link barked and lunged, held back only by their harnesses. Kyle stepped in front of them, blocking their view. "Calm," he said. What effect the words had were soon redoubled when Kyle held both hands in front of him, palms down. Slowly, because the dogs were still excited, but surely every dog on his team lay down. *If only the dogs obeyed so easily on the trail when they were at full speed, the wind and the cold biting at their eyes and ears*, Kyle thought.

Ewan walked up behind Kyle, toward his dog.

"Stop," Kyle said. Ewan stopped as if under the same control of the dogs. "King, come."

King's muscles loosened, and his bristled ridgeline relaxed as he walked next to Kyle and sat down.

Ewan grabbed his dog by the collar and led him toward the rest of the team, tethering him back to his neck line in his patch of straw. Kyle knew that even in Ewan's anger, he'd be gentle with the dog, as every musher held one thing true above all else: they loved their dogs. So the young husky's punishment was a mild lecture, a good rub down, and some hot stew. And despite the tension between Kyle and Ewan, the toils of the trail required respect between the two. At least until the finish line.

There was movement near the checkpoint entrance, where Jed had asked the reporters to wait. One reporter had found his way back outside, and his curly blond hair stuck out conspicuously from behind his camera. Huey lowered his camera and made eye contact with Kyle for several seconds, and King took several steps forward. Kyle looked down at King and back up at Huey. Neither moved.

"Come on, King," Kyle said. The dog followed him to the sled, and Kyle clipped him back to the neck line.

For the next hour Kyle tended to each of his dogs. Massaging them, feeding them, making sure they were hydrated and healthy.

What was left of a pail of hot water ironed the air next to Kyle with drops of steam, and he marveled about his dogs' performance. They had made it over some of Alaska's toughest peaks, through frozen tundra and places where many men had never heard of, let alone wandered to. Temperatures had tested their tenacity on the stretch from Eagle to Central, wind their will atop American Summit, and the darkness their determination on the many nights they camped under the stars in anticipation for the next run.

Yet when Kyle saw Jenna walking toward him, it was just a small bump in the snow that got him.

His right boot stuck in the ground, clipping a hard pile of snow, and he tripped. The snow felt more like wet sand against his face. Mixed with dirt, it was grainy and brittle. Kyle rolled over onto his back and looked up at several strands of red hair that bunched together and scrunched out from underneath a striped beanie.

"Well, that was impressive," Jenna said.

Kyle let out a deep breath and closed his eyes. "I don't think I can get up."

"You know, there is one thing I'm starting to learn about all mushers."

Kyle squinted up at Jenna. All he could focus on was her lips. They were slightly pursed and covered in a thin sheen of lip gloss. He didn't know where this feeling came from or why, but he wanted to kiss her. Instead he pushed the thoughts back to a place he rarely visited.

"What's that?"

"That most of you give off this persona of being so rugged and fierce in the face this white wild, but deep down"—she squatted next to him—"you're all just big babies."

"Can this baby just rest here while you check out the dogs?"

Jenna's eyes widened, and her lips parted. She removed one of her wool mitts and knelt and pressed her hand against his forehead.

Kyle felt that familiar cool touch from before, the same feeling that washed over him when he sank his feet into the ocean on a hot day. He tried to hide the fact that chills just ran throughout his entire body.

"What are you doing?"

"Checking to see if you have a fever."

"Why?"

"Because until a few hours ago, your only reputation was that of a dog-crazy rookie musher."

Kyle forced out a tired smile. "I'm a changed man."

"Are you saying that you trust *me* with the dogs?"

"Well, I'm technically less than a foot from them, but yes, I trust you...if you'll just let me lie here for a few minutes."

"Okay, but all kidding aside, you're really okay, right?" Jenna said.

"Yeah, just tired."

"You know those reporters are filming and taking pictures of you right now? They'll probably have some fantastical headline about how you collapsed at the checkpoint."

Kyle rolled his head back until he saw several Steese's Roadhouse windows filled with cameras. Jed was pushing Huey back inside.

Kyle pointed his right arm behind him toward Huey and Jed. "You see that young reporter with Jed?"

"Yeah," Jenna said. "That's Huey. He cracks me up. He's like a walking bottle of caffeine."

Kyle cupped his hands around his mouth and let loose a shrill and deafening caw.

Jenna jumped back. "What the crap was that?"

"Ha-ha, sorry," Kyle said.

Huey came running over, Jed chasing after him.

"Yes, Mr. Walker?" Huey said, standing over him.

Kyle waved off Jed, who was out of breath after a few steps in their direction. "How'd you know I was calling you?"

Huey looked around, as if maybe the answer were behind him. "Umm, I don't know. I just, uh...I don't know."

"Miss Maynor here could use a hand with the dogs."

Jenna looked down at Kyle, confused, but took his cue. "I could? I mean, I could. But"—she pointed at Huey—"no questions."

Huey ran his pinched fingers across his mouth like a zipper and then grunted, "Mmmi mmomise mmot uh mord."

Jenna rolled her eyes. "Come on. Mr. Walker needs his beauty rest. Oh, anything I need to know about the dogs?"

"Umm, yeah, Ria's front leg is wrapped. I think it's just muscle soreness."

Jenna stared blankly back at him.

"Sorry. Ria is the female still on the sled, with Artemis." As Kyle said that, King curled up to Kyle, his neck line pulled taut. Kyle unclipped him and wrapped his arm around the lead dog.

"Okay, I'll check King last," Jenna said.

Kyle moved his right hand through King's thick fur as Jenna walked to the sled. He leaned closer to King and then quickly turned away. "Holy cow, King. You smell worse than hog crap drying in the sun."

King twisted his head around like a parrot and looked back at Kyle out of the corner of his eye. "Yeah, I know. I probably stink too."

13

HUEY STOOD behind Jenna and scribbled furiously into his notepad while Jenna worked. Just a couple steps away, she noted that Kyle's eyes were already closed and his stomach rose and fell with a sleeplike breath. She had seen other mushers drained and dragging at late stages of the race, but she was worried Kyle was letting it consume him.

Can he keep going like this, she thought. She didn't yet know him well enough to answer.

A dog—Story, her collar tag said—licked her face, stealing her attention away from Kyle. "Okay, okay, I see you."

Two snow hooks were cinched in a straight line, about thirty feet apart. Kyle had unclipped the tug lines but left the dogs connected to their neck lines so they could spin around and curl up in the straw. All except for Ria and Artemis, who were still clipped to the basket of the sled.

Story was the only dog not lying down. She was the left-hand swing dog, paired with—Jenna checked the next dog's tag—Link, and positioned directly behind King when they ran. Story's tail wagged, and her body wriggled as she greeted Jenna.

"How do you have so much energy left?"

Jenna ran her hands over the seal-like hair on Story's forehead and down the nape of her neck, where her coat thickened. She was black, except for a large white bow-tie marking across her chest and some tan markings above her eyes and toes. "You are a very beautiful dog, yes you are. But would you lie down for me?" Jenna pointed to the ground, and Story instantly lay on her side. "Wow, that was quick."

Each dog was akin to an ultra-fit endurance athlete, and so the first thing Jenna checked was Story's heart rate. After that she lifted the skin on the back of Story's neck, and it popped back to its normal position immediately, suggesting good hydration. Story wagged her tail through every check, and that in itself was the next check: attitude. Jenna kneaded her fingers around Story's ribs to check her weight. She scanned over eyes, mouth, nose, and ears. Then she spent a couple minutes at each joint in Story's legs.

About ten minutes later Jenna moved over to Link, then Shyanne and Spirit, Hali and Sunshine, Giza and Gardens, Colossus and Olympia. All the dogs, except Link and Story, were curled up next to each other, their tails wrapped around their faces. Story was sitting down but still watching Jenna's every movement, while Link rested off to the side, as far away as the rigging would allow.

Ria sat up, her ears pressed flat against her head when Jenna reached the sled. "So I know why you're back here, but what about your friend Artemis here?" Jenna said. "Kyle didn't mention why Mr. Artemis was back here." Jenna looked at the young female. "This wouldn't happen to be your boyfriend, would it?"

Ria barked.

"Yes, he is very handsome. You are a lucky girl."

Ria barked several more times.

"Okay, okay, calm down. Let me just take a look at this leg of yours."

Jenna unwrapped the neoprene that ran the length of Ria's foreleg. She didn't see any inflammation or soreness, no knotted muscles or unusual striations. "I don't know if your daddy wants me to walk you, but I need to see you put a little weight on this leg."

Jenna squinted at Kyle, but he hadn't moved even the slightest.

She unhooked Ria's neckline from the sled, and Artemis' head lifted up. "Don't worry. I will bring her right back. I promise."

Holding the rigging like a leash, Jenna guided Ria out of the sled and onto the packed snow. "Easy now," she said. Ria wasn't favoring one leg more than the other.

"I think Mr. Kyle might be a little more cautious than he lets on," Jenna said as she clipped Ria back into the basket. "Is he like that with more than just you guys?"

Ria curled up next to Artemis and rested her head calmly on his croup. She looked up at Jenna with her glassy black eyes.

"He's a mystery to you too, huh? What about girls though? I bet he's got a lot of ladies after him back home." Ria didn't move. Jenna laughed softly to herself. "Yes, I'm fully aware I'm trying to have a conversation with a dog, but that seems to be par for the course lately."

She stood up and strolled toward Kyle. King, curled up next to Kyle, lifted his massive triangular head when she stepped next to him. She held out her hand, and King sniffed at it.

"You know you're going to be famous."

King barked.

"Shhh," Jenna said, holding her finger up to her lips. "He needs his beauty sleep. I'm just going to take a quick look at you, okay?"

"I wouldn't do that," Kyle said, his eyes still shut.

It was too late though. Jenna reached down toward King's paw. He bared his teeth and let out a coarse growl.

Not prepared for that, she fell from her squat to her butt.

"I told you," Kyle said.

"How do you think I'm going to check him out if he's going to bite my hand off?"

Kyle rolled onto this side and put his arm around King, like he was cuddling him. "Who, this little guy? He's harmless."

King tilted back and licked Kyle's forehead. "See?"

"Seriously though," Jenna said. "I really do have to make sure he's fine."

"He's fine," Kyle said.

"Okay," Jenna said. "Let me just make some final notes here—musher...not...cooperative...reco...mmend...he drrropps...lead dog."

Kyle sat up on his knees. "All right," he said. "You win. All you have to do is say the magic word."

"The magic word?"

"Yeah, but don't say it too loudly."

"You know it's like three degrees out here, and you're joking about magic words?"

"What? No. There's really a magic word. But I'll have to whisper it in your ear."

Jenna tilted her head to the side.

"Well, I can't just say it out loud. It's—"

"Magic?"

85

"Exactly." Kyle made his way around King on his knees and whispered the word in her ear.

She laughed. "That's it?"

"Try it," Kyle said.

"I just say it?"

"Yup, followed by whatever command you want. Like sit, down, or stay."

"I can't believe I'm doing this." She shook her head and looked at King. "Cheese." King sat straight up, and his ears perked, and ten feet away, Link did the same.

"I told you to whisper it. This is some powerful stuff you're messing with here."

"Stay," Jenna said.

King didn't move.

"Now he's not going to bite me?"

"I trusted you," Kyle said. "Don't you trust me?"

That's always the question, Jenna thought. *Always.* She reached out her hand toward King's paw, but the dog didn't move. Jenna ran her fingers around the pads of each paw and up his front legs to his shoulder. "Down," she said. King plopped down to his side, and Jenna inspected his back legs and feet.

Kyle tossed King a treat from his jacket pocket when Jenna finished.

"See," he said. "Magic. Now let's go inside. It's freezing out here."

14

AFTER THE REPORTERS realized Ewan and Kyle were too exhausted to answer any questions, most left for Circle City or Two Rivers. Central became the emptiest checkpoint Kyle had seen on the trail. While Kyle and two others had made it here in nine days, some mushers wouldn't make it here for another four or five, if at all. After a rather hilarious phone call with his boss, Huey had convinced him the story was still at Central. So other than a couple that seemed attached to Ken Ellis, Huey was the only reporter that remained. And for now he sat alone across the room, punching the keys on his laptop.

Two ceiling fans lit most of the space with artificial light, while a strip of black tracking lights finished it off. Just below them, Ken Ellis was talking to a younger man in glasses, scribbling on a notepad, while a girl in a pink beanie held a boom pole just inches from Ken's face. He looked tired and worn down. Even his clothes clung to lines and creases of exhaustion. His team left Whitehorse wearing bib number five, and while he'd only passed four other mushers, he'd yet to relinquish his lead.

Kyle and Jenna took an empty booth on the edge of the restaurant.

"He's done," Jenna said.

Kyle lifted his bib suspenders off his shoulders and let out a groan as he rotated each of them several times. "What do you mean?"

"He just dropped six dogs."

"He can still finish with eight," Kyle said.

Jenna shook her head. "He only came in with eleven. He'll be one under the required six to finish."

"Why so many this time?"

"CIV," Jenna said. "Canine influenza virus."

Mushers didn't like to hear about viruses on the trail. They were contagious. They could spread. They took time to heal, and no one really knew where they came from. Food, bowls, collars, leashes. Kyle wasn't too worried though. He'd checked each dog at every stop. They were eating well, active, no coughs, no problems with eyes or noses.

"That just leaves you and Ewan. And Ryne, but he's down to just nine dogs now," Jenna said.

Kyle searched the room. Ewan was sitting at a high-top with four people around him and three tape recorders splayed across the table.

"He's only dropped one," Jenna said. "You'll each have thirteen going out tomorrow."

It was early afternoon, and the mushers had an option of an eight-hour mandatory layover at Central or at Two Rivers, about sixty miles away. The smart play was to go out when Ewan went out. Draft him as long as possible, and then burn right by him at the end. That was what most mushers would do.

That wasn't what Kyle would do.

He knew his team like the moon knew the stars. He would take his eight hours now, but not just eight. The dogs needed more rest, so they'd stay until daybreak, or just before, when the temperatures were just coming out of their low points.

"I think they want to talk to you."

The same two people who had stayed with Ken Ellis left Ewan's table and were sitting a couple tables away from Kyle and Jenna. They glanced over at Kyle several times and ventured over.

"I think you're right," Kyle said.

The girl in the pink beanie smiled, and the man pulled a tape recorder out of his pocket.

"One question," Kyle said, holding up his finger. "Then I've got plans."

The man looked like a rabbit trying to do a crossword puzzle. His nose scrunched up in confusion, and lines of thought creased across his forehead. It looked like he was considering wasting his question on what plans Kyle could possibly have. Instead he asked the same question every reporter asked. "What is a Carolina gray?"

"It's a dog," Kyle said.

Underneath the table, Jenna kicked Kyle in the shin.

"Owwww." Kyle reached down and rubbed his leg.

Jenna tilted her head forward and raised her eyebrows.

"The Carolina gray is a landrace breed, still wild in some parts near the Savannah River. The gray comes from DNA evidence that these dogs, who came over during the Bering land strait migration, likely descended from a line of Korean Jindos and bred with native gray wolves."

Kyle returned the tilted head and raised eyebrows to Jenna, accompanied by a self-satisfied smile. "Good enough?"

"And how did you come upon the breed?" the man asked.

89

"That would be question number two. Like I said, I've got plans. Catch me in Fairbanks, and I'll answer all the questions you want."

The man clicked off his recorder and pushed it into his front pocket. "Okay...umm...thanks. Oh, and good luck."

"So you've got *plans*?" Jenna asked.

"Well, I was hoping to talk to this girl for a little bit tonight, but she's turning out to be rather violent."

"Like I said earlier—you guys are all babies."

Kyle started to get up from the table. "I guess that means you're busy..."

"No," Jenna said quickly. "I mean, me and my sleeping bag did have some pretty big plans."

Just below the window sat rows of white sacks with mushers' names scrawled across them in marker. They were drop bags the mushers had packed ahead of time. Kyle had already emptied one full of dog food, and he knew another contained some supplies and sealed bags of food for him. But after the past week of dry teriyaki chicken and rice, or bacon and potato soup, the last thing he wanted right now was more trail food.

"Are you hungry?" he said.

"I'm always hungry."

"All right, let me take care of a few things, and then I'll be back."

* * *

Jenna watched as Kyle exited the facility, and she wandered to a window. His steps were light and happy, like his dogs. Most of them stood to greet him, but Kyle pressed them to lay back down and rest.

He picked up their food bowls and made a final pass with some water. He checked each dog's harness where it attached to the neck line, and tugged on the gangline to make sure it still held firm in the snow.

Jenna snuck back to her seat.

Once back inside, Kyle peeled off his outer layers—anorak, gloves, boots, and socks—and draped them over the booth.

Jenna looked down at Kyle's bare feet. "Aren't you cold?" The floor was probably near forty degrees.

"To be honest, the best part of every checkpoint is taking off my socks," Kyle said. He put his foot on the bench next to Jenna. "They feel like waterlogged footballs after standing on the sled for hours."

Jenna scooted to her left. "Eww, gross!"

"So, that's a no go for a foot massage later?"

"That's a never go," Jenna said. "Feet freak me out."

Kyle inched his foot closer, and Jenna slid to the end of the booth until she hit the wall. "Kyle!"

Kyle laughed. "Okay, okay," he said. "Be right back."

She straightened up in her seat as Kyle walked over to the kitchen counter on the other side of the checkpoint. He leaned forward against it and stretched out his calves and rolled his shoulders. His thermals weren't skintight, but they were tight enough that Jenna could see the tension release from his toes all the way up to his neck.

Her eyes traced the muscled outline of his legs and landed on...a pair of thick-rimmed black glasses and two cups of steaming-hot cocoa. Huey was standing directly in front of her.

He handed her the warm mug and sat down across from her.

"I don't think Kyle is in the mood for any more questions right now," Jenna said.

Huey pulled the rectangular spiral notepad out of his front pocket and grabbed the pencil that was perched behind his ear. "I read this book once," Huey started, "that said the single most important question you can ask someone is, 'If you were given the opportunity, would you take it?'" Huey sped along in his energetic way. "I don't think that's a good question. Do you think that's a good question?"

Jenna didn't have time to answer before Huey moved. He started scribbling something down as he talked. "No, it's not a good question. Well, it's a good question, but it's not a great question. I came up with a great question though. See, I've got this theory that everything in life requires sacrifice. And sacrifice is not a fun thing. In fact, it's a painful thing. But it's an important thing. And so it becomes the one factor every person must eventually ask oneself."

Huey stopped writing and looked up at Jenna. His cadence slowed. "What in life is worth the pain? And what in this race is worth the pain for Mr. Walker?"

Jenna was taken aback by the question. Huey was right. It was a great question. And before she knew she was speaking, two words escaped her lips: "His dogs."

Huey spoke as he jotted something down. "I think you are right, Ms. Maynor." Then he looked at Jenna and said it one more time before Kyle interrupted them. "I believe Mr. Walker thinks you are too."

Kyle walked up with a tray full of food. "Sorry, Huey. I can't do any more questions right now. Going to get some food and then some sleep."

"Sure thing. No questions today, Mr. Walker. Just thought you two might like some hot chocolate." Huey motioned to the white mug sitting on the table, still steaming.

"Yeah, thanks," Kyle said.

Huey walked back to his messy stack of backpack, laptop, and jackets, and Kyle sat down.

"That was nice of him," Kyle said.

"Yeah," Jenna said, nodding. "You could say that."

Kyle set the tray down, watching flavor waves rise from the food.

"Did you just order one of everything on the menu?" Jenna said.

"I thought you were hungry," he said with a grin.

"I think your definition of hungry and my definition of hungry might be slightly different."

Kyle picked up his plastic fork and held it out like a teacher with a pointer. "Well, we've got pizza, sweet corn, pulled-pork sandwich, some rolls, and...red and brown soup."

"Red and brown soup. Really?"

"It's not red and brown?" Kyle said.

"It's lentil and sausage," Jenna said.

"Okay, red and brown lentil and sausage soup."

To Jenna's surprise, they ate the entire tray of food. What Jenna didn't eat, Kyle finished off.

Kyle hadn't spoken much during their meal, which was fine, but Jenna was full of questions. Mostly about the dogs, about the breed—Carolina gray. *Like the reporter had asked, how did he discover them? Why do they make good sled dogs?* Jenna cupped her chin in her palms, her mind sifting through questions, finally hovering over one she had to know the answer to.

"What about King?" Jenna said.

*　*　*

Kyle wiped away a ring of water from his eyes. They burned with exhaustion, and he knew, whether he wanted to or not, he had to get some sleep soon.

"What about him?"

"He's…different from the others. Please don't take this the wrong way, but he's protective to the point that worries me a little."

"There's a lot to it," Kyle said. He yawned involuntarily.

"I'm sorry," Jenna said. "You know your dogs better than me, and you need some sleep."

Kyle folded his anorak into a squarish pillow and jammed it between the back of the booth and the window. He leaned his head against the goose-down insulated fleece, closed his eyes, and began to speak. "I don't know why for sure. I mean, King's always been different. He doesn't look at the sunset and wonder why the sky is full of blue and orange—he just knows it should be. He doesn't know why the clouds open up and drop down rain—he just accepts it. Some of the other dogs are similar. Like Ria and Story, Spirit and Artemis. And Biscuit back home. They just look at the world differently."

Kyle exhaled all the air from his lungs, letting loose the tension in his shoulders and chest. "When I was younger, when I first found King abandoned in the woods, I didn't really know much about dogs. So part of it, if not all of it, is my fault. I was only thirteen or so when it happened." His words faded, and for a moment he didn't speak.

"What happened?" Jenna asked.

"There were five of them," Kyle said. "Some of the details are blurry, like, I don't know why we were walking there that day. We just were."

Kyle's eyes were still closed, and his words escaped his lips at the same rhythm as the rise and fall of his chest. "King knew before I did. I don't think he smelled it or heard it. I think he felt it. I think it called to him like a song from the forest.

"They weren't large gray wolves of the south—more brush wolves, or coyotes. All of them smaller in size than King, but fierce in the way nature makes the wild. Several of them were coated in the fresh blood of a fawn that they were ripping and tearing at. It was the closest I'd ever been to seeing an actual kill. Even since then I haven't seen anything like it. The entire scene was shocking, and I felt trapped, frozen.

"I didn't hear a growl or see a flash of teeth. I just saw movement. Two of the coyotes were on us, so quick. You just don't understand the speed of nature. It's not like what you read about or what you watch on television. There's a savagery that I can't explain."

Again Kyle paused, and again Jenna asked, "What happened?"

"I don't remember it all. One minute the coyote was on top of me. I can still feel the blood-stained fur that clumped between my fingers as I grabbed at his neck. I remember his sticky breath, and then the bite."

Kyle rolled up his red sleeves and rested his right hand on the table, palm up. He flexed, and a raised scar flexed with him, from his wrist to about midway up his forearm. "I think I yelled something or screamed out. And then King barreled into the animal. They rolled together for several feet, long enough for me to get up and run.

"And so I did. I ran. I was clutching my arm as I ran, until I heard this sound. It was somewhere between a scream and a growl. Somewhere between angry and afraid. I turned around and saw them on King. They snapped at his legs and feet, clawed at his face. He looked up at me, his master, his best friend, his brother. And that same noise that was somewhere between a scream and a growl, somewhere between anger and fear, enveloped me.

"I sprinted back towards him and knocked the two on top of him into a tree with my shoulder. I kicked at them, threw dirt at them. Anything I could. King sprang from his back, and moved...moved like...something possessed. He intercepted one that leapt at me and flung it to the ground, lunged at another's throat, and swerved back onto a third.

"His heavy coat, covered in dirt and moss and grass and blood, heaved with his thick breaths as he circled me. His mouth foamed with an incessant flash of fangs. The coyotes scattered soon after, and he fell down on top of me, his paws on my chest, and his knowing eyes stared straight into my soul."

* * *

Kyle didn't see it because he was already falling deep into the place of dreams, but a single tear streamed down Jenna's face. And she understood.

15

THE MAIN ROOM of Steese's Roadhouse stayed well lit even late in the night. Jenna rolled over in her sleeping bag that was tucked against the wall, and the nylon ripstop crinkled below her. She'd checked in Ryne Moore's dogs about four hours after Kyle fell asleep, and Frank Lesh's team about an hour after that. After news that the next musher was at least five hours out, she'd curled up in her sleeping bag for a few hours.

When she woke, she checked out the bench against the window, but Kyle wasn't there. Knowing he hadn't planned to leave until closer to dawn, she scanned the room. Of all people, Kyle was sitting across from Ewan "the Hammer" Harbinson.

How long had they been sitting together? What were they even talking about?

Jenna stood and arched her back slightly as she retied her ponytail. She pulled on her left boot, balancing on her right foot, and then tried to slip on her right, all while trying to watch Kyle and Ewan. It didn't work. Her right foot missed the boot, and she fell forward, stubbing her toe on the chair in front of her. "Shit!"

Every person turned in her direction. She held her hand over her mouth in embarrassment and limped over on her left foot to bend down and pick up the boot she'd dropped. Holding it up, she said, "Sorry."

They all went back to their business of sleeping, or eating, or whatever they were doing. All except Kyle. He sat turned halfway around on his stool and watched her. His expression was blank, but his eyes were moving over her body. From her feet, up the tight jeans on her legs, over her waist, across her chest, and finally he rested on her eyes. She was shocked how insecure a single look made her feel.

Kyle looked back at Ewan, said something to which Ewan nodded, and then walked out the front door. *What just happened?* Jenna ignored the current of frigid air that eased into the room and finished putting her boot on. She looked down at herself. At her jeans, at her belt, at her jacket. *Did I do something? Is he mad at me? Okay, stop. It was just a look. I don't care anyway. Okay, fine, I care, but...*

Before Jenna could finish arguing with herself, the door opened again, and Kyle walked back inside. He blew into his bare hands, wiped his shoes on the soaked brown welcome mat, and walked over to Jenna, who was sitting at a table in front of her sleeping bag, boot still in her hand.

Kyle sat down across from her. "You all right?"

Jenna tightened the laces that wrapped only around the ankle of each boot. "Yeah, why?"

"Either that chair said something rude, in which case it had it coming, or you just hate old furniture."

"You know how mean those old chairs can be."

"Oh yeah, tell me about it."

They both laughed.

"For a minute, I thought you had left," Jenna said.

"No. When you so elegantly addressed the room, it reminded me of something."

"What?"

"Shit."

"No, I mean what did it remind you of?"

"Let me rephrase—dog poop."

"So I remind you of dog poop? Watch it, buddy. You saw what I did to that chair."

"No. I meant I needed to make sure the dogs were...relieving themselves without any problems."

"I suppose I can accept that as a valid answer."

"Anyway," Kyle said. "Anything exciting happen while I slept?"

"Ryne Moore checked in. I think he's out sleeping in that storage shed they turned into bunks. And Frank Lesh came in behind him." She motioned over to the table where Frank was sitting, stirring a bowl of something hot.

"Shouldn't you get some more sleep?" Jenna held up her watch. "It's only four or five hours until daylight."

"I slept for about six hours," Kyle said. "Probably the best sleep I've had in the past ten days."

"Folded up in a hardwood booth?"

"Now you've got something against the booth too?" he joked.

"You should have seen me yesterday. Me and that booth really got into it."

"I would have liked to," Kyle said.

Kyle's comment threw her off. His demeanor was somewhere between serious and playful, but he managed to hide it all behind a calm facade. "So, what now?"

"Is that a Western Mountaineering Bison GWS sixty-degree sleeping bag?" Kyle said, pointing behind Jenna.

Jenna turned around in her chair to look at whatever Kyle was pointing at. "What?"

Kyle walked around behind her, bent down, and ran his fingers over the Pertrex lining and the full down collar.

Of all things, my sleeping bag impresses him...

"I bet you never get cold wrapped up in that," he said.

If you only knew.

Jenna sat down next to Kyle, who was still staring at her sleeping bag. She leaned back against the wall of logs and stretched her back against their curved ridges.

"You don't mind if I join you, do you?" Kyle said.

"Of course not."

Kyle sat down next to her and stretched his legs straight out in front of him.

"So what was that all about?" Jenna said.

"What was what all about?"

"You and Ewan."

"Oh, we're going to go out together for Eagle Summit."

"Together? You and Ewan?"

"Yup."

"And who's idea was this?" she asked.

"Actually, it was his. He said the last place you want to get caught alone is on Eagle. He was going to go out with Ryne, but obviously that's not happening anymore."

"I feel bad for him," Jenna said.

"Ewan?"

"No, Ryne."

"Oh, yeah."

"You don't?" she asked.

Kyle shrugged. "I don't know. I mean…I suppose I do, but I try not to think about it."

"Does it bother you? That he had to drop so many dogs?"

"Not really."

Jenna watched Kyle. He averted his eyes from her and looked across the room, as if scanning some great distance. He wore an old trucker hat with a white fishnet back and navy bill, which seemed to be his standard when he wasn't wearing a beanie. Even then she could see his hair was cut short and cropped neatly around his ears and neck.

He bit down on his lip, and she noticed the unshaven jet-black hairs that filled his face. He was attractive in both the conventional sense of symmetry and tight lines around his jaw, mouth, and eyes. And in the unconventional sense there was an effortlessness, a breath of underlying wild to him. Like maybe he was born in the lowlands of South Carolina, but he belonged in the free-roaming Yukon. She really didn't care he was just nineteen. She went to prom with a junior when she was a senior. One of her best friends married a guy three years younger. Even Demi was forty-one when she started dating Ashton Kutcher. There was something about him, regardless of age, that intrigued her endlessly.

"Why do you do that?" Jenna said.

"Do what?"

"You did it back in town when I asked about your home, and while you told me the story of King and the coyotes. You turn your eyes away, and even though it's out in the open, it's like you're trying to hide from the truth."

Kyle's brown eyes met hers with a certain peace. It wasn't a still and tranquil peace like that of a lake in midsummer, but forced. Learned. Like that of a man who had come to terms with life even though he didn't agree with everything it had to say.

"I like it when you wear your hair in a ponytail like that," he said.

Jenna couldn't help but smile, and still his eyes haunted her. "I'm guessing that works on all the girls back home?"

"I wouldn't know," Kyle said.

Jenna tilted her head, as if to prod him into the answer. "Oh, come on."

Kyle ran his fingers over the tight space between his ears and hat. For the first time since she met him, he looked nervous. *Maybe he's not hiding anything*, Jenna thought.

"I'm sure there's lines of girls waiting for Mr. Kyle Walker."

"None that aren't covered in black-and-white fur."

"I'm sure Olympia, Ria, Hali, and Story wouldn't mind."

"Ria might."

"Okay, but seriously, I find it hard to believe Kyle Walker is still on the market."

Kyle pushed himself off the floor, leaving Jenna alone on the sleeping bag. "I'm going to go check on the dogs."

"Didn't you just check on them?"

Kyle didn't respond. He just started walking toward the door.

"Kyle," Jenna said, getting to her feet. She took several steps after him. "I didn't mean anything by it."

He looked back at her before he opened the door, and in that moment Jenna realized it wasn't peace or fear that glazed across his eyes. It was fear. And the weight of it struck Jenna like nothing before.

16

SEVERAL HOURS LATER a coarse voice woke Kyle, curled up on the bench.

"I'll see you at the base in an hour."

Kyle opened his eyes. Ewan Harbinson.

He looked over to the blue sleeping bag in the corner of the room. Jenna wasn't there. A couple reporters were eating breakfast or lunch or dinner, depending on how terrible their circadian clocks had been thrown off, and one of the handlers was sleeping sitting straight up in a chair. But Jenna wasn't there.

Kyle straightened the kinks out of his socks so they felt flat against his skin, laced up his boots, and pulled on his beanie and anorak.

His dogs sat at the sound of his boots crunching over the snow. They were rested. They were ready.

Less than thirty miles away, the sun yawned, and morning's first light splashed across the tips of Eagle Summit to the east. At the lower elevation where Kyle was, it was still too dark for shadows. He ran through the ritual of checking the dogs quickly while clipping their harnesses back to the towline. They cheered in excitement for the day. Even King, who sang his song above the rest.

Kyle clipped him in last. He held King's big head between both hands and spoke to him like he understood each and every word. "Take it easy this morning. We have an easy thirty until the base of Eagle. We're going to walk most of the way up with Ewan's dogs. I don't want any trouble."

King barked.

"No," Kyle said. "We're not running up the mountain."

King barked again.

"I don't care if you can do it. It's too much energy wasted. Plus somebody could get hurt."

King unfurled a catlike sound. "Yes, we can let loose on the backside."

Several of the dogs jumped forward, restrained only by their harnesses and the claw brake buried in the snow.

"Calm," Kyle said. They barked and pulled to the left, and Kyle saw Jenna walking toward him.

He left King and walked around to the back of the sled. The basket was strapped in tight, and instead of Artemis and Ria, there was a little extra fuel and food.

Jenna stopped in front of the sled, next to Colossus and Olympia. "You heading out?"

Kyle nodded, and she walked around next to the sled. She placed her hand on the top rail, and it felt as if she had electrified the sled. Every part of his body shivered.

"Okay, well, I just wanted to say good luck, and I'll see you in Fairbanks."

Kyle nodded and pulled the brake line. Before he spoke, the sled lurched forward, the natural pressure of the dogs to pull against any restraint, carrying them slowly past Jenna. He looked at her from the slit in his balaclava. Even in the dark he found himself drawn to every aspect of her. The way she pressed her lips together, the strands of hair from underneath her headband and parka. Even how she stood, the length of her body forming slender lines. He ignored all of it and looked to King. "Hike, King. Hike! Hike!"

* * *

Running sled dogs was much like sailing a boat on the ocean. The horizon seemed ever distant and ever present. No musher could rely on a feeling to guide him. In the vast sphere of wintertide, it was the dogs guiding mushers, and mushers the dogs.

Ewan was waiting a little past the base of Eagle, about a fifth of the way up the mountain to the second pitch, where the slope started to sharpen. Kyle stopped behind him and looked around at the blushing sky.

"What is it?" Ewan said.

He remembered Doc's words from when he was a kid: *Red sky in morning, sailor take warning...*

A single goshawk cruised below the rose-hued clouds.

"Nothing," Kyle said. "Let's go."

Kyle dropped two brakes and gave the command for his dogs to stay. They weren't going to like this part, but it was necessary. Both of the men started to walk Ewan's sled up the east face of Eagle, leaving King and the others to wait their turn.

Soft snow of the mountainside meant more friction on the runners and heavier pulling for the dogs. About twenty yards up the mountain, Kyle looked back to his dogs. Most were barking and jerking on the gangline, trying to do anything but sit there. Kyle ignored the others for a moment and kept his eye on King, who was looking to the west, his head angled to the sky and his nose sniffing violently at something.

105

A sudden wind surfed across the mountain back, and King's fur lifted and shuddered at the blast of air. He looked straight at Kyle and then arched his back, throwing his head into the air and letting out a shrill cry. This red morning was different than the others—it was apparent to Kyle that King knew something he didn't.

Kyle let go of Ewan's sled and stopped walking. Then he felt it, as did the rest of the dogs. It fell from the sky like an anvil and smashed into the team like a train.

"Get to your team, now!" Ewan growled. "And get to Central!"

The wind nearly knocked Kyle from his feet, and he caught himself as his gloved hands found the snow. Running in boots and a trans-Alaskan suit was hard enough. Running down a mountain of spongy snow with gusts of hurricane-force winds was nearly impossible.

He stumbled twice again before reaching the sled and then took a hard roll past when he lunged for the brake. King was turning the sled before Kyle had ushered a single command. Kyle tore the brake from the trail and flung it into the sled as the dogs took off back down the mountain.

The sky to west dropped a wall of white behind them, and the maroon morning gave way to the black once again.

Bits and pieces of the storm ambushed the teams as the wind lifted the soft snow to the west and blew it across the trail. The frozen air slammed into them, biting them, whipping the dogs into another gear. In a matter of seconds the trail was gone, and all Kyle could do was aim the dogs at Steese's Roadhouse still visible in the distance.

Kyle looked back, but zero visibility blocked any discovery. He couldn't see the summit or Ewan's team. Even the sky hid behind the blinding white. Kyle worried the violent storm might beat his team to Central.

"Hike, King! Hike! Come on, Colossus!" He yelled in futility as the storm stole his words.

They were upon Central sooner than Kyle expected. He threw out both brakes and stamped them into the ground. The door in front of him swung open, and someone yelled. There was no time to discuss it. Hopefully, they knew he was taking the dogs inside.

Ewan pulled in right next to him but drove his dogs straight to the door without hesitating. He unclipped the towline from the sled, ignoring the sled entirely, and started shouting at the dogs to keep moving inside.

People were trying to pull the teams in, but the lines of over twenty dogs were tangled, which spooked the dogs. Kyle saw Jenna among those trying to help, holding on to King's collar. He pushed Colossus and Olympia inside, and Ewan came barreling in behind him. Someone shut the door, and his hearing returned, but the looks of fear spreading throughout the checkpoint screamed louder than the storm itself.

17

IT TOOK SOME TIME, but they finally got the dogs untangled and separated. Ewan had jarred his shoulder pretty badly when he forced his way into the checkpoint, and he sat across the room with his dogs and a warm blanket draped across him.

Kyle's team sat opposite Ewan, stretched out along the wall adjacent to the front door. Ryne and Frank were hunkered down in the book room that was a small wooden structure separate from Steese's Roadhouse. In between Kyle and Ewan were a myriad of tables, filled with Huey and two other journalists; a vet tech named Wendy; Tom, wearing a camo hat and behind the counter; and the checkpoint manager, Ronald, whom everyone called Jed, for reasons Kyle didn't know.

Jed sat alone with the television remote control in one hand and a satellite radio in the other. He flipped through the channels on both devices, but ironically got nothing but static and snow. They had lost communication with the other checkpoints, and with both Whitehorse and Fairbanks.

They knew nothing about the storm, except that every so often the wind hit so hard that even the walls flexed against its weight. Occasionally Jed unbolted the storm shutters, which were really just pieces of plywood on hinges and bolts, and peered outside. It was useless though—there was a uniform illumination of dusty snow from the ground to the sky. It wasn't just a blizzard. It was a whiteout. And Kyle and the others were a little unsettled that they had no warning of it.

Jenna sat on the floor between Story and Link. Story's masked face rested on her feet, while Link sat straight up in her lap.

"Got some new friends?" Kyle said.

Jenna shifted behind Link and tilted her head so she could see Kyle. "He won't stop shaking," she said.

"He's pretty much a big baby." Kyle snapped his fingers. "Come here, Link." The dog shuffled off Jenna's lap and plopped down right on top of Story. She grunted at the added weight but accepted her role as a literal safety blanket.

"Are they okay like that?"

Kyle crawled closer to the wall and sat down next to Jenna, both of them pressed up against Story and Link. "Yeah, this is the assumed thunderstorm position back home."

King stood up and turned in several circles until he recurled in a position facing Kyle.

"I think he's jealous," Jenna said.

"No. He's just wondering why I keep sitting by this other human."

"And why do you?"

Kyle brushed several clumps of ice stuck to his pants. He could feel the vertical lines of Gore-Tex stitching against his nails, and it sounded kind of like a zipper.

"You can say it," Jenna said. "I mean, I know I'm just so awesome."

Kyle looked at her, but he wasn't laughing with her. "I've never had a girlfriend."

"What?"

"You asked earlier, and I kind of just walked out."

"*Kind of* walked out?"

"Okay, I walked out without answering, because…it's embarrassing."

"You're telling me you haven't dated a single girl back in Bishop Hill?"

"Bishop*ville*," Kyle said.

"Bishop Hill sounds so much cooler…but I still don't believe you."

"Well, there's Belle. She's absolutely gorgeous. And then there's Jade, very exotic. Then there's Biscuit."

"Biscuit?"

"Yeah, Biscuit."

"You actually know a girl named Biscuit?"

"If you don't believe me, just ask Story. Right, Story?" Link had moved from atop her, and she lifted her head.

"You're describing your other dogs…"

"I told you I don't date. Geez, you don't gotta rub it in."

"Okay, well, what do you do back home then?"

Kyle squeezed his right wrist and spread his fingers, flexing his hand several times. The gas pockets in his joints crackled and popped as he rotated his wrist in circles.

Jenna reached for his hand. "Stop that." She spread his hand out over her leg, palm up, and pressed her thumb into the padding around the base of his fingers. She pressed between each joint until she reached his fingertips, and then she squeezed with an even force. It sent pangs of relaxation all the way to his elbow.

"My days are mostly the same. I'm up with the dogs early and with them until noon, training, grooming, feeding, et cetera.

110

After noon I usually take one or two for a walk around the farm, and if they need to work on anything in particular, that's when we'll do it."

"The farm?"

"Doc owns a couple thousand acres, sandwiched between lots of farmland."

"And Doc is…"

"My uncle."

"So every day, all year long, you're with the dogs."

"Well, no. There are some days Doc needs help around the farm or something. I read a lot too. Doc usually grabs something when he's in town."

"Fiction, nonfiction?"

"A little bit of both. For some reason he's been bringing home some poetry books lately. What about you? You really like doing this?"

"Well, I'm not out here freezing my patootie off, sitting in a shack in the middle of the Yukon, just to prove I'm Alaskan."

"Your pa…tootie?"

"Yes. My patootie."

Kyle reached down and pet King, who had been inching closer since they started talking. He unclipped King's neck line, and the dog stepped between Spirit and Shyanne and sat down on Kyle's left side. Kyle ran his hand through King's fur and rested it gently over his chest.

"Why do you do that?" Jenna said.

"Do what?"

"Place your hand over their chest like that. I've seen you do that with several of the other dogs too."

Kyle hesitated, searching for the words to describe something innate to him. "Everyone can sail in smooth waters or dance when the music is playing. The great leveler is how you respond when the music stops. And you'll find that the answer is here." He pointed to King's chest. "It's here where the melody hides, where it has hidden since the first day you opened your eyes."

"Those poetry books must be working," Jenna said, winking.

Kyle continued to pet King. The familiarity of running his hand across his dog's soft black fur was relaxing. It was something he had done for years.

"What makes King so special?"

"Imagination," Kyle said. "Every dog is special. Many are separated by physical attributes. The speed of a greyhound, the strength of a mastiff, or the agility of a collie. It's nothing short of majestic. But King has something else entirely. He's faster, stronger, and more agile than almost every sled dog out here, but it doesn't separate him the way his mind does. He intuits commands that I haven't taught him, understands words by their mere cadence. But it's more than that. It's hard to explain."

The conversation went on like that for several hours. The dogs slept, and Jenna asked question after question after question. And then so did he. There was probably no point in the past nineteen years that he had talked more than with Jenna, but trapped inside a checkpoint in the middle of a blizzard, there wasn't much else to do.

Until King's ears perked just milliseconds before a large thud boomed at the door. Having become accustomed to the sounds of the thrashing storm, Kyle didn't move.

Thddd.

Again the noise rattled the door, and again Kyle—along with the others—ignored it, except King, who stood. He lowered his eyes and glowered at the din that clanged like a branch striking against the steel hinges.

Story stood behind King. She lowered her head and straightened her back and tail until her body stiffened like a nocked arrow. Ria and Artemis also rose, staring down the oaken door, and across the room several of Ewan's dogs stirred.

Kyle and Ewan both spoke to the dogs in their own secret language, but King would not be placated. Several sinusoidal growls emanated from deep within his stomach. Kyle stood next to him and watched the front door swing open and a man fall through the threshold, blood stained across his forehead and face, and the storm screaming behind him with unending resolve.

18

KING LAUNCHED FORWARD at the unwelcome stranger, and the gangline whipped through the table it was tied to. Two chairs went flying, and the bulky table toppled over into the next. Story and Link joined King, pulling toward the door, and nearly swept Kyle off his feet.

Ewan's dogs also charged at the man, unleashing their potential energy like springs coiled and waiting. Ewan tried to get in front of them, but their gangline also drug across the floor, clipping two high-top tables and spilling their contents over the checkpoint.

Kyle watched Colossus and Olympia pull from the other end of the line, and then like a row of dominoes, all the dogs were barking and yelping and pulling toward the man who struggled to get to his knees.

Kyle dropped to one knee and brought his hands together like a man bending to pray. He sucked in the frigid air around him and blew through the slit formed by his two thumbs. A screaming whistle shot through the room like an old steam train signaling its presence. As fast as everything started, it stopped. Even the storm seemed to subside in those brief moments.

Jenna covered her ears in clear preparation for the next onslaught.

"Sit," Kyle said.

Jenna slowly lowered her hands.

Some of the dogs whined in excitement or anxiety, but they all sat. Behind Kyle, all of Ewan's dogs also sat. With the room hushed, they all turned their attention back to the man at the door. He pulled the door shut behind him and lifted the fur-covered hood from the rest of his face. He was Inuit, and he was hurt badly.

Jenna rushed around Kyle's dogs and over to the injured man, who appeared to struggle to even hold himself firmly on his knees. He was bleeding from a gash on his head, his hair matted in blood and snow. When she reached him, he started mumbling words in a mash of different languages that came out like a garbled gasp for breath.

Kyle followed behind Jenna and grabbed the man by the left arm, trying to help him to his feet. For the first time, the man's voice was clear, but laced with hesitation, and he spoke in what Kyle guessed was the old language of the Inuit. "Ataneq amaruq." The man pointed to a place behind Kyle. A place along the wall, where only King was standing. Where King was watching. "Ataneq amaruq," the man said again. And then he collapsed back to the floor.

Kyle looked back at King and then up Jenna. "What did he say?"

Jenna knelt by the man and placed her hand in the space between his shoulder and neck. "He's unconscious, but he has a pulse." She moved her hand over his nose and mouth. "And he's breathing."

"What did he say?" Kyle said again.

Before Jenna could speak, Ewan took several steps forward, as did the checkpoint manager, who was standing next to Ewan. "Ataneq amaruq," Ewan said. His eyes locked on Kyle's. "King of wolves."

19

THE MAN LAY motionless on top of a table, his chest rising and falling, and Jenna cleaned and bandaged the wound across his forehead. The others gathered in a semicircle, watching her every move.

Questions floated around unanswered. *Where did he come from? What happened to him? Who is he?*

Ewan broke from the group and started back toward his dogs.

"Where are you going?" Kyle said.

"There's no use watching the man sleep," Ewan muttered.

Huey walked over to the table. "Anything you need me to do, Mr. Walker?"

"Why are you asking me?" Kyle said.

Huey shrugged, "I don't know. I just thought..."

"I'll see if I can get some bags of ice from the back," Tom shouted over them.

Huey ambled back to his table, his head down, his pen moving rapidly across his notebook.

The checkpoint manager looked at Jenna. "What do we do now?"

"Aren't you the one in charge?" Kyle said.

"Yeah, but...but I'm not a doctor," Jed said.

"She's a vet," Kyle said. "Unless this guy is covered in fur, what do you think she's going to do?"

"Kyle," Jenna said. "It's okay." She glanced at Jed. "I'll watch him for now. Once he's awake, we'll need Ewan to translate."

Jed put his clipboard down on the table, the same clipboard he had clutched since Kyle first saw him yesterday. "Okay, I'm going to see if Tom needs any help with that ice."

Once Jed was through the kitchen door, Jenna said, "You don't have to be such a jerk."

Kyle didn't even try to defend himself. He was frustrated. He wanted to the storm to pass and to be back on the trails. He wanted to know what the man meant by what he said. And he also wanted to know if Jenna wanted to maybe catch a movie and dinner when this was all said and done.

"Sorry," he said.

"Good, now hand me my tweezers."

"What?"

Jenna pointed to her medical pouch next to his right hand. "My tweezers," she said again.

Kyle looked down at a clear plastic box and flipped open the clasps on each side. Inside, the tools looked similar to the ones Doc used back home. There were different-size forceps and clamps, needle holders, and there in the top right corner, tweezers.

He handed them to Jenna and watched her pull several long slivers of something from another wound that had ripped through the man's jacket, down to his forearm. She laid the pieces on a napkin.

"What is that?" Kyle said.

Jenna held one piece in front of her. "It looks like…like wood."

* * *

After about an hour, Kyle paced along the wall. He listened to the wind huff around the building like horse's breath heavy against the ground, and watched their new addition lie alone on the table.

Jenna had been tending the man's wounds the entire time, but now she set her tweezers on a nearby table.

Kyle walked over to her, and Jenna sat back halfway on the edge of the table, exhaustion in her eyes.

"You think anyone else got caught in the storm?" she asked.

Kyle let out a deep breath and tried to relax his shoulders. He paused in his pacing and drummed his fingertips on the table. "I don't know. Probably. It was on us quick and without any warning." He watched Jenna's reaction and added, "But I'm sure everyone's all right."

Jenna nodded and quietly said, "Yeah."

"Hey, uh, what's your favorite restaurant?"

Jenna smiled. "My favorite restaurant?"

"Yeah, King wanted me to ask."

"He did, huh?"

"Yeah, he said you promised to take him to your favorite restaurant after the race was over."

"Oh, right. Well…hmm…probably the Crepery."

Kyle squinched up his nose. "Okay, how about your second-favorite restaurant?"

"You don't like crepes either?" Jenna said.

"No, I do. It's just King, he's not that big on crepes."

119

"Oh, right, King…okay, well…then I think I'd have to go with the Cookie Jar. They have these breakfast burritos that are ahhmaaazing."

Kyle scrunched up his nose again.

"Do you like anything?" Jenna yelled.

"King prefers most food to have no flavor. The closer it tastes to cardboard, the better," Kyle said.

The worry that had faded returned when Jed reappeared from the back.

"How's he doing?" Jed stopped midstride to stare at the man's still form.

"He appears to be stable for now," Jenna said. "The cuts on his forehead and arm were bad. It's hard to say how much blood he lost, but I think he'll be fine. Probably need to get some antibiotics in his system soon though."

"And we don't know anything about him?" Jed asked.

"Ewan thinks he's a local Inuit, probably from one of the cabins near the base lakes around Crazy Mountains."

"That's just crazy," Jed said behind an uncomfortable smile.

Kyle stared blankly at the poor joke. Jenna shook her head.

Jed twitched, his right hand gripping tightly to his clipboard and his left squeezing the life out of the satellite radio.

"Have you heard from anyone yet?" Jenna said.

Jed looked down at the black walkie-talkie in his hand and pressed the channel scan function. Nothing but static and silence screeched through.

"Okay, well…" Jenna started, shoving away from the table.

"I'll let you know if I hear anything," Jed said before he sped back to where Tom was standing, fiddling with the television again.

Jenna turned to Kyle. "Now what do we do?"

"Wait," Kyle said. "We wait." He resumed pacing at full speed.

* * *

They didn't have to wait long. A few minutes after Jed left, another static sound screeched through the room—the Inuit man gasping for breath as he sat up. He felt down the arm where his jacket had been cut away and wounds bandaged, and then ran his hand over the gash on his forehead, covered up with tape and gauze.

A few of the dogs barked as he moved his legs around the side of the table.

"I don't think that's a good idea just yet," Jenna said, stepping up to him and placing a gentle hand on his shoulder.

Kyle and Ewan stood behind Jenna, and Jed peered at the Intuit from a few feet away.

"Do...you...speak...English," Jenna said.

"What?" the man said. "Of course I speak English."

"Okay," Jenna said. "Well, I guess that's settled."

"Do you remember you name?" Jenna said.

"Kallik." And at the sound of his own name, a switch obviously flipped within the man. "My wife! My children!" he screamed. He pushed Jenna back, planted his feet on the ground, and fell forward. A chair from the adjacent table broke his fall.

Kyle and Ewan scrambled to lift the man back onto the table.

"I told you not to do that," Jenna said. "You've lost blood. You're hurt. You need rest."

Kallik struggled against Kyle and Ewan, who lightly held on to his shoulders to prevent him from getting to his feet again. Huey even ran over to help hold down the man's legs.

"They need help," Kallik said, his eyes scanning the room, as if searching for the way out.

Jenna looked up from Ewan to Kyle. "Who needs help?"

"My wife, my daughters."

"Where are your wife and daughters?" Jenna said.

"Trapped," he said, trying to tug out of Kyle's and Ewan's hands.

"Trapped where?" Jenna said.

"What?" Kallik said. He appeared to be in and out of a conscious state.

"Where are they trapped?"

"By a tree near our cabin, one mile past where the river splits around the mountains."

"That's almost five miles from here," Ewan said. "There's no way he ran that in this storm."

"They're trapped!" he screamed. "Please. You must help!"

"What is ataneq amaruq?" Kyle asked.

The question seemed to calm the man for a moment. He pointed over to King. "The ataneq amaruq. The king of all wolves."

So Ewan had been right. Kyle glanced back at King sitting against the wall. His triangular ears were standing on end. King was silent, but his almond eyes met Kyle's, and they spoke in an old language that man once knew. A language that used to bind man to nature. A language that Kyle still clung too.

"Why did you say that when you first got here?" Kyle said, still maintaining a light hold on the man's arm.

Kallik relaxed slightly and stared straight at King but spoke to Kyle. "He ran to me in the night. In the storm. He guided me here. From the Summerland."

Kyle let go of Kallik's arm, where blood started to seep through the bandage, and he swung his arm wildly, hitting Jenna a few inches below her shoulder.

She fell to the side against Huey and grasped at her left shoulder.

Before anyone could respond, Ewan reared back and punched the man square in the jaw, just below his nose. The man's head jerked back, and he fell flat against the table. His arms splayed to each side, and his legs crooked over the table corner.

"I've had about enough of that," Ewan said.

Kyle unclenched his fist and looked down at the man. Long black hair, the color and feel of grease, was tied with a leather wrap. His face was unshaven except several patches along his jaw, where scars showed through. *Ataneq amaruq*, Kyle said to himself. It almost felt like the words themselves contained a drip of magic.

"What was that all about?" Jenna said.

"Sounds like a bunch of hogwash to me," Ewan said. He walked to the window and lowered the wood shutter just enough to see out. "There's just no way he made it that far in the storm. You've got a better chance of getting kicked by a snake."

"What if it's not?" Kyle said. "What if he's telling the truth?"

Ewan clasped the shutter back and walked past Kyle toward his dogs. "It don't matter. Ain't nothing we can do in this."

Kyle felt Jenna's eyes boring into him as he stood there staring at the man on the table, and then over to King.

She had clearly interpreted the look on his face. "You're not going out there."

Kyle looked up. His eyes narrowed, and his chapped lips clamped down.

Jenna marched the four steps over to him and shook his shoulder lightly. "Kyle. You're not going out there," she repeated.

"We can't just leave his family out there to die."

"Kyle, we don't even know if they are out there, or where."

Kyle repeated the words of Kallik. "His wife and daughters, by a tree near their cabin, one mile past where the river splits around the mountains."

"And where is that? Show me on a map."

Kyle left Jenna standing alone and strode over to King.

She followed behind him and this time lowered her voice. "Kyle, please. I know you want to help. I don't like the idea of his family stranded alone either. But…you just can't go out in this."

Kyle walked over to his sled and started to inspect the runners and rails.

"What if you can't find them? What if they're gone?"

"I'll find them," he said.

"How?" Jenna asked.

He unzipped the basket, and several items clanged together like pots and pans.

"How?" Jenna asked again.

Jenna looked at Huey to back her up, but he shifted his eyes to the ground. "Huey, come on."

She turned to Ewan, who was watching this unfold from across the room. "Ewan. Tell him. Please."

Ewan stroked the ears of one his dogs resting across his legs. "He's not that stupid."

Jenna closed her eyes as Kyle spoke.

"I leave at dawn."

20

BY THE TIME dawn came, the storm had subsided. The clouds still hung tightly to the sky, reflecting a gray light across the tundra, but the snow had stopped, with only a little over a foot piled up near the door.

Jenna had pleaded, yelled, begged, warned, and even flirted with Kyle in her attempts to prevent him from leaving. None of which worked.

Ewan stood next to her and watched Kyle and his dogs fight through the fresh powder. "Youth has everything," he said. "Everything but age."

Jenna hadn't seen this side of Ewan. The edge was gone, and he looked almost regretful. But she didn't care. "If anything happens to him, I'm blaming you."

"What? Me? I'm not the idiot who…"

"You're the idiot who could have stopped him!" she screamed.

Jed tapped Jenna on the shoulder.

"What!" she yelled, turning on him.

Tom and Huey were standing with him.

"I…I spoke with a few other checkpoints. Seems like service is back up."

"And?" Jenna said.

"Well, good news is not a single musher or dog was reported injured."

Jenna turned back to watch Kyle's team disappear into the trees. "Hopefully it stays that way."

Jed tapped Jenna on the shoulder again.

"What?" she said.

"There's more."

Jed looked around to Tom and the reporter, who hung their heads. "The storm is building."

Jenna looked at the clouds and the distant horizon. "It looks like it's clearing up though." She pointed out toward Eagle and several other peaks. "You can even see several summits. The clouds are clearing."

"I'm just letting you know what I was told. Fairbanks has suspended the race until this passes and wants everyone to stay inside for the next twenty-four hours."

"Who did you talk to?" Jenna said.

"Cody."

"Cody Stratham?"

Jenna snatched the radio out of Jed's hand. "How do you work this thing?"

Before Jed could reply, Jenna depressed the push-to-talk button. "Cody? Please come in, Cody."

Several static beeps later, a man's voice responded. "Go for Cody."

"Cody, this is Jenna out at Central checkpoint. Can you give me a weather update?"

"I just talked to Jed. Aren't you with him at Central?"

"I am, but could you just repeat the update to me?"

"Well, we're expecting a category-three storm moving in over the next six to twelve hours and lasting up to twelve to twenty-four hours."

Jenna let the radio go silent. Ewan, Jed, and Tom stood, frozen in place, listening.

"Copy?" Cody said.

"We have a problem," Jenna said.

"Yeah, I know. It's not ideal, but y'all will be fine for another overnight at the checkpoint."

"It's not that," Jenna said. "We have a musher and his team outside."

"Well, get them inside," Cody said.

Jenna was thankful she'd made Kyle take Jed's backup radio.

She switched channels and called out for him. "Kyle, do you copy?"

They waited.

"Kyle Walker, do you copy?" she said again.

The clouds rattled and shook as thunder boomed in the distance. The muted sky flashed and began to swell again, and the once tired and yawning white morning turned a bleak gray.

"Kyle!" Jenna yelled. "Kyle!"

Ewan peeled the radio from her grasp. He switched channels, and his jagged voice spoke. "Cody, this is Ewan Harbinson. We can't reach our musher."

"Please repeat. You are breaking up," Cody said.

Ewan clicked down the microphone, but the communications were already starting to sound like nothing but fuzz.

A new voice spoke across the radio. "Ewan, this is Ranger Art Fisher. Can you please repeat?"

Jenna left the radio with the men and walked back inside the building to her empty spot along the wall and slid down until her knees were tucked to her chest. She fought back the feeling of tears in her throat and bit down on her bottom lip.

"He's gone."

* * *

Early on the trail, the snow was thick, and the dogs jumped as much as they ran. Kyle watched them as they took a trail out of Central. It wasn't littered with orange-painted lath to mark the way, but something else about it seemed foreign, unexplored.

He thought back to dog sledding as a boy. During the day he scouted Doc's property in wheeled sleds through thousands of acres of switchgrass, dirt, and live oaks. At night he sat with King by a small fire, even in the summer, and read books like *Call of the Wild*, *Winterdance*, and *Stone Fox*. He read aloud to King the great adventures of Balto and the race to Nome, and stories of the unadulterated wild by John Muir.

"Gee! Gee!" Kyle yelled instinctively.

He thought back to everything he had learned about the laws of the trail. And he began to repeat it over and over in his mind. *Remember that the wind can take heat away from your dogs at astonishing rates, even if the temperatures are relatively mild and the dogs have thick coats. Consider putting dog blankets on your upwind dogs* [in this case, the dogs on the right side of the gangline] *before you head through an operating blow hole. Expect some soft trail. Be prepared for significant overflow sections. Always move forward. Always. Even when fatigue drags your heart down into your feet. Move forward.*

The trail can be overwhelming at times. Don't look at it as a whole. It's not a thousand miles. It's one mile, and then another. The nights will get the best of even the calmest minds. The red fox that will run alongside you at daylight, and that particular blue in places when crossing the ice of the Yukon River will give way to the howls of gray wolves and the endless black silence that fills the space between the stars.

In the event of storm conditions, travel with a partner...

Kyle lingered on that last bit before he finished.

In times of high stress you can choose to believe the worst, or you can choose to believe the best. This is what defines success on the trail. The brave musher is not the fearless, but the one who has faith in himself and his team.

The river split in two, and King slowed the pace, but Kyle kept the team to the trail. *Another mile*, he thought.

Overhead, the sky began to grumble, but the clouds still scattered away from the mountains. Yesterday's storm seemed to be passing. The sled rattled beneath his hands, and even through his gloves he could feel the rough tape, like dry snakeskin.

To his left a cabin came into view. From a few hundred yards out, nothing looked out of place. It wasn't until they were right up next to the cabin that Kyle saw the gaping hole on the right side. The entire side wall had been ripped off.

"Easy," Kyle said. "Easy." The team slowed to a stop, and Kyle tossed out the brake line and stomped it firmly into the ground.

He clomped over to the cabin and placed his hand along the back corner where the wall used to dovetail together. It was a clean break vertically down to the ground. Nature had unmade what man once made. There was one problem: the wall wasn't just torn off—it was gone.

Kyle looked around. To the right, in front of the cabin, stood a shack. Maybe for drying meats. Behind him and to his left was nothing but more snow-covered spruce and several evergreens breaching the surface.

He checked the other side of the cabin where the wall was still perfectly in place. Again nothing.

Several of the dogs barked and yipped from behind him, up on the trail. He turned around, and a teenage girl stared right at him. Her dark-brown eyes burned into his. Her slender, firm body was lined in caribou skins, the fur facing out, except her fur-trimmed boots, which looked store bought. The girl's skin was a pale white, her cheekbones high and defined. She looked in her teens, but she didn't look Inuit.

But one question would confirm everything. "Is your father Kallik?"

The girl nodded.

She was surprisingly calm, possibly still in shock, Kyle thought.

"I'm Kyle, a friend of your father's," he said. "Is your mother okay?"

The girl shook her head, and as Kyle approached, he noticed two water-stained lines down each cheek. "Can you take me to her?"

"I tried," she said. The words quavered off her tongue. "I tried to help them."

"It's okay. Where is she?"

The girl marched toward the trail, and Kyle followed.

"Wait," he said. "What's your name?"

"Faith." She uttered the one word while striding forward, not even looking over her shoulder.

She led him across the trail and down into a switchback to a copse of several giant trees, and in front of them lay the splintered and missing wall.

On the ground next to the timber was an axe, the half-broken blade in the snow. Kyle felt the grooves and fragmented wood in the wall, where the blade had been swung several times. Rays of light crept between the gashes, and below the boards, Kyle saw two more pairs of eyes. One pair belonged to a little girl, no more than three or four, clutching a small wooden paintbrush, the bristles blue and brittle. The other set of eyes stared up at him, the women clutching a spear-like piece of timber that had been driven straight through her right leg.

"It makes her feel safe," the woman said.

Kyle looked at the woman.

"The paintbrush," she said. "Her father gave it to her. It makes her feel safe."

He nodded. "I'm Kyle."

"Mallory," the woman said. She placed her hand on the little girl's shoulders. "This is Tera."

"Is she injured?"

"She's scared," Mallory said.

"Okay, just hang tight for a few more minutes."

He stepped back and looked at the wall jammed into the trees. It was splintered but solid, and luckily the top part was not more than six feet off the ground. He reached in his jacket and pulled out the radio. A yellow light blinked on top. "Central, this is Kyle Walker. Please come in."

No response. "Central, please come in."

No static. No broken voices from the other end. Just silence.

"Central, this is Kyle Walker. Please come in."

Faith's eyes caught his, her fear palpable.

"It's all right," he said. "I can get them out with the sled."

Kyle slogged to the side of the runners and snapped an unusual command. A command he rarely used but that his dogs knew. He pulled the handlebar tight until the gangline was also tight against the dogs. "Colossus, back!" The dog looked at him somewhat confused. "Back!" Kyle said again. Colossus picked up his red-boot-covered paw and took a step back. Then another. And another. The other dogs followed suit, and Kyle kept pressure on the sled, pulling it back to take up any slack in the line. The dogs backed up the sled until Kyle was close enough to latch the claw brake over the top of the wall.

Kyle yelled through the wooden structure. "Take cover. I'm going to pull this thing down."

"Line out, King." This was the difficult part. Kyle wasn't concerned with the dogs' ability to pull this thing down. He was pretty confident the claw would stay latched. But he was worried if they pulled too fast, the bottom might kick back at the girls. The problem was, it would take power to pull the wall down. But he couldn't use speed. The dogs would have to pull slow but hard. And as well trained as his dogs were, as well trained as King was, there was no command for that.

21

THE SNOW FELT like gravel where Kyle knelt in front of King. "We're going to do things a little bit differently today."

King tilted his head and looked lengthwise down his nose. Not to hear Kyle better, but to see him. To see Faith, who stood next to Kyle.

"What can I do?" she said. Her voice was stolid, her dried tears wiped away.

"Talk to your sister," Kyle said. "Make sure she and your mom are okay. Just reassure them."

Faith nodded, and she walked back to her family and knelt beside them. "Everything is okay, Tera. We're going to get you out real soon."

Kyle turned his attention back to King. "Calm," he said, the closest command to slow he had.

King relaxed, the anxiety for the run shrugged away in his coat. The other dogs watched, as they always did. King took his cues from Kyle, but they took theirs from King.

Kyle backed up several steps, sure to stay directly in front of King. "Come," he said.

King walked forward, followed by Story and Link and the rest. Until the gangline drew tight. Like King never knew he was harnessed into the sled, he looked back and whined.

"Calm," Kyle said, afraid King might suddenly lunge forward and jerk the wall down. "Come."

Again the lines strained and stretched until their fibers creaked, and the dogs whimpered. They didn't understand why they couldn't break free and pull against the resistance with all their might. They were confused.

Kyle took two more steps back. "Come. King, come."

He watched all his dogs dig their paws into the ground and lower their bodies. They stuck out their necks, and Kyle could see the strain in their eyes as they fought against their own nature to pull harder. Ria, his youngest, jumped forward and barked.

"Easy," Kyle said. "Easy, girl."

The dogs continued forward until there was no give left in the lines, and the misplaced wall moved. It groaned and wiggled as the dogs marched. Kyle's eyes moved from the timbers that trapped Mallory and Tera to his dogs. In all of his training with them, this may have been the single moment he was most proud. It was a magnificent sight to watch the dogs pull in unison but to withhold the incessant fight to drive the sled. To tame a fire that would elude many for a lifetime.

The structure fell and stamped out the snow beneath it. Link jumped as the wall knocked the wind out of the ground, and Kyle ran to where Mallory lay. He noticed a stream of burnt-red snow below her. The wound was worse than she let on.

"Mallory," Kyle said. "I need to put you on the sled."

Her head tilted to the side and rested stiffly against the trees behind her. She made an indiscernible noise.

Kyle looked back at the little girl, Tera, who sat completely still next to Mallory, clutching that paintbrush to her chest. He knew nothing about children. *Do they talk at this age? Will they understand me?* He was clueless, but explained anyway. "Tera, I'm going to move your mom over to the sled. You stay here. Okay?"

Tera blinked.

"Okay…" Kyle reached his right hand underneath Mallory's legs, and his left wrapped around her shoulders. He tried to keep her pierced leg completely still as he lifted her, but it wasn't possible. She screamed out in pain.

This is only going to get worse, he thought. "Hang in there." Kyle took several steps up the short incline to the sled. He laid her down on the sled and surveyed her wound. Fresh blood saturated her pants around her leg, but he could do nothing. He knew every vibration from the sled would disturb that jagged strip of wood embedded in her leg and send striations of pain shooting through her body. He tried the radio, but again was met with silence.

He tucked the radio back into his jacket pocket and found Faith standing next to him, holding Tera's hand. "What's wrong?" she said.

"Nothing, was just checking in. Letting your dad know that we'll be on our way back soon."

"But they didn't answer?" Faith said.

Kyle hesitated. "Umm no, but I mean, that's normal way out here." He looked at the two girls standing next to the sled, next to their mother, and realized he had yet another problem. There was no way he could take all three back on the sled.

Mallory's legs were already spilling over the front. There was just enough room put Tera on her lap, but even then with Mallory slipping in and out of consciousness, he would have to tie them to the basket. Where could he put Faith?

136

He looked down at the rear runners at the place where the neoprene footboards were screwed to the wood. There was three inches of extra space. Normally he'd put Faith on the footboards and stand behind her. Even if he had to stand on his toes for the trip back, it would be fine. Except for one thing: Mallory.

With Faith on the back, it changed everything. The balance, the weight, the speed. If they rocked too hard on a turn or skirted through a rough patch of ice and flipped the sled, that would be potentially fatal for Mallory. Even with King at lead, there was a good chance the dogs wouldn't stop immediately, if at all, before dragging a tattered and broken sled back to Central without them.

"Let's get your sister up on the sled," Kyle said.

He and Faith lifted the little girl so that she was sitting on the left side of her mother's lap, away from the wound, away from the blood.

Kyle pulled out a spool of static rope. "Can you let her know that I have to tie her in, and it may be a little tight?"

Faith bent down and spoke softly to Tera as Kyle wrapped the rope around her waist and chest, double-braided like a seat belt. Mallory tried to wrap her arms around her daughter, but they kept falling to the side, so Kyle had to tie them around her. That was the easy part though.

He looked up at Faith. "I can't take you." The words came out wrong. "I mean, I will have to come back for you."

"I know," she said.

"Stay in the cabin. It shouldn't take me more than an hour or so, and I'll be back."

Faith nodded.

"Are you cold? I can start a fire real quick if you want."

"I'm fine."

Kyle looked around at the situation once more. The woman and her daughter tied to his sled like meat. The dogs waiting anxiously. The cabin exposed and alone. He hated this. He couldn't just leave the girl.

"Come here," he said.

Faith followed Kyle toward the front of the sled. Toward King.

"Have you been around dogs?"

She nodded. "My dad used to run dogs when I was younger."

"This is King," he said.

Faith held her hand out just inches from King, until he leaned in and sniffed it, scenting her. King's mouth parted, and his pink tongue tasted her caribou overmittens. This was not his normal reaction to people, but Kyle knew it wouldn't be. He could sense the wild of the Yukon in Faith, so King could sense it even more.

He unclipped King's neckline and harness from the team and said something he thought he'd never say to anyone. "I'm going to leave King here with you."

* * *

The weather was a fickle old man. Sometimes it seemed to follow certain habits, and other times it, well…it didn't. This was one of those other times.

Kyle and the dogs moved through a series of natural wind tunnels as they charged back to Central. He fought the balance to run the dogs hard, knowing it was better to run them safe while Mallory and Tera were in the sled.

They passed through several blow holes that swirled in localized hurricane-force gale winds and blew fat snowflakes across them, bits and pieces sticking to their clothing and stinging their faces.

Kyle didn't think anything of the intermittent winds. There were places on the trail where it could be twenty and sunny, and only a mile away negative twenty and walls of gray. It wasn't until they broke free from the forest and into a plain of white. When Central came into view. It wasn't until he looked to the west—when God clapped his hands, and blinked his eyes, and pulled back the curtains of the storm in the distance, and cried out once more.

22

THE DOOR TO Steese's Roadhouse opened, and Kallik came running out. Kyle watched him as he tramped through the snow toward them. He looked down at Mallory and Tera still tied to the sled.

For the first time the little girl spoke, screaming something in Inuit at the sight of her dad. But Mallory lay still, except for the soft bounce of her hands and shoulders that matched the cadence of the team's gait.

Jenna and Ewan followed Kallik through the door, followed by Jed and Huey.

"Easy, Link! Easy, Story!" Kyle said. They pulled to a stop, and Kallik tripped toward the sled. His knees ricocheted off the side brackets and shook his wife and daughter.

Whether it was the sight of dried blood around the stake in his wife's leg, the way her head slumped to one side, or even the rope cinched around her body, Kyle didn't know. But something triggered Kallik. He clawed at the simple square knots around his daughter's body.

The dogs, uneasy with his presence, barked and growled.

Kallik's knees and feet wriggled and kicked near Colossus and Olympia as he struggled to free his daughter.

"Kallik," Kyle said. The man was too focused to respond.

"Kallik, I'll untie them, but you've got to calm down."

It was as if Kyle hadn't spoken. Kallik tugged haphazardly on the ropes. "Where's Faith? Where's my other daughter? Where's Faith?"

Jenna ran over to Kyle and hugged him, then took a step back and hit him on the shoulder. Before Kyle could respond, Olympia squealed under the weight of Kallik's boot. Kyle grabbed Kallik by the shoulders and pulled him back. He squared up to the man and looked him right in the eyes. "You've got to calm down. We need to get your wife medical attention."

For a moment Kallik relaxed, and Kyle released the ropes and lifted Tera out of the sled and handed her to Kallik. He hugged and kissed the girl as she threw her arms around his neck, dropping the blue paintbrush to the ground.

Ewan plopped down an orange stretcher next to the sled. Kyle looked over and nodded thanks.

"On three," Kyle said. He had hold of Mallory's arms, and Ewan had hold of her feet. "One...two...three." They lifted Mallory as little as possible and slid her onto the stretcher.

Just like before, she screamed out in pain.

"On three," Kyle said again. "One...two...three..."

Mallory's eyes shot open and then shut again as she gasped. Kallik set Tera down and fell alongside his wife, knocking Ewan over backward. The bottom of the orange stretcher thudded to the ground.

"Kallik!" Jenna yelled. "They're trying to help. You've got to let them get her inside."

Thwak. Ewan's fist barreled into a combination of Kallik's jaw and shoulder for the second time. Kallik grunted but shrugged it off.

141

"Stop!" Jenna yelled, but her hollow voice had no effect.

Story and Link barked, followed by Colossus, Olympia, and Ria. Jed ran into the fray, trying to pull Kallik back so Kyle and Ewan could get his wife inside. Jenna was still speaking, but her voice was drowned out by the dogs.

A shudder of fear swept through Kyle's body. The tingle started in his neck and stopped when it resided deep within his chest. He released his grip on the stretcher and turned to face the woods he had just come from.

"Stop," he said.

Everyone ignored him.

Above the noise behind him rose another sound in the distance. A familiar sound. "Stop," he said again, louder. Kyle closed his eyes and angled his ears toward the sound, but the clang of foolish people drowned everything out. He turned on them and shouted like a man possessed.

"Sttooopp!"

The shouting died off, and even the dogs paused in their barking.

His chest rose and fell from the sudden onslaught of his lungs. His heart palpitated loudly in his chest, but in the distance that familiar sound returned.

Everyone heard an ice-like howl float across the checkpoint.

Jenna looked at the team of twelve dogs as they responded. Story and Link jerked their heads to the sky and howled. Followed by Spirit and Shyanne, Ria and Artemis, Giza and Gardens, Hali and Sunshine, Colossus and Olympia.

They all joined in to respond to their leader, who wasn't among them. To respond to the call from the wild.

To respond to King.

23

MOST OCEAN WAVES were caused by the wind. The rich blues and foaming whites looked beautiful as they crashed in from the Pacific and washed across the shore.

Snowstorms in the Yukon weren't like that. They rolled in like waves on the back of invisible currents, but in place of the rich blues and whites was a roil of dirty gray, like someone had shaken out a doormat over the clouds. And there was anger. Unrelenting, unbiased anger. This was the image Kyle saw to the west as he watched the sky assault every space that filled his eyes.

He ran alongside his dogs and checked each of their harnesses, tugging on the rigging and clips. He unclipped Link from the lead with Story and walked him back to where Ria stood. Link was a good swing dog with Story, behind King. His calm cooled the fire that pushed Story, but right now Kyle needed speed. He clasped Ria next to Story and walked back behind the sled.

"Jed!" Kyle yelled.

Jed snapped into motion and took several steps toward Kyle.

"Help Ewan and Jenna get the girls inside. Call it in to Fairbanks. If they don't respond, try another checkpoint. Do whatever you have to, to get them help."

"O-okay," Jed said.

"What are you doing?" Jenna said. The lines across her face moved with confusion and questions. "Where is King?"

"He's with Faith."

"Who is Faith?" Jenna asked.

She didn't understand, and Kyle didn't have time to explain. But her presence stayed him. His eyes traced the countless blues in hers. They caught hold of several strands of red hair underneath her jacket and followed them down her soft white skin.

A strange feeling danced around his heart and stomach, like the coming dawn, and for a brief moment, all he wanted was to stay with her. Just to be near her, just to talk to her.

The sky bellowed. Story barked, and Ria leapt forward.

Jenna put her hand on Kyle's arm, and that warmth of the morning sun returned. "You're not going back out there."

"I'll be back," he said.

"Kyle, this is serious. You can't go back out there."

"I'll be back." He clapped his hands together twice, and the sled moved forward. "I promise," he said. And then he gave the usual command. "Hike, hike!"

* * *

The winds pressed in against them as they bounded back toward the woods. Kyle could feel the drop in temperature of the approaching storm, even through his fur-lined overcoat. Last night's fresh snow was a welcome hindrance as Story and Ria led the team. Without King or Link up front, the sled bounced and trembled with reckless speed. But speed was all Kyle cared about right now.

One mile, two miles, three miles. They trucked through the tundra at a furious pace, running straight into the face of the storm.

Kyle did the math in his head. Each mile took four to five minutes. They'd reach Faith and King within the next fifteen minutes. With King back at lead, even with the added weight of Faith in the sled, they could make it back to Central in a half hour.

Forty-five minutes, he thought. *Come on.* Kyle yelled to the dogs, spurring them on. "Hike, hike! Come on, Link! Come on, Spirit! Let's go, Ria!" He clapped his hands. Even if they couldn't hear the snap of one glove against the other, they could sense it. Like a whip held just inches above a horse's back, the dogs knew, and they jolted forward.

Four miles, five miles. Past the fork in the river and up a steep bank to the highland trail over the cabin. They were just minutes away.

And then Mother Nature, like the cruel temptress she could be, listening to his very thoughts, changed everything. A violent wind whipped across the trail and lifted the snow like a white blanket tossed about on a clothesline. Colossus and Olympia slowed, and like a domino, so did the rest of the dogs.

Kyle used his arm to shield his eyes. Small clumps of snow clung together like ice chips and harassed them. The tips of trees that lined the trail bent and broke in the wind, and Kyle ducked as a branch flung past him. At first it felt like the wind gusted in front of them, and then it pushed from behind, and Kyle fell forward next to Link.

The trail to the cabin sat too high up. They were exposed, and in a matter of seconds covered in the storm. Kyle rushed forward and grabbed hold of the gangline between Story and Ria and pulled them forward, down a three-foot drop and into a copse of trees. It wasn't a smart move, but it was the only option. The sled flipped over behind them, and he fell against a hollowed-out trunk.

It sheltered his front side as Kyle scrambled toward it. The dogs followed, dragging the tipped sled along the bottom of the slope. He pulled the dogs close to him and laid his head against the log. Even with the added adrenaline, even with the shelter of the dead tree to his back and the dogs covering him on the front, he shivered.

I should have waited, he thought. *King would have been fine. I should have stayed with Jenna.* But then he thought about Faith. Kyle was prepared to camp at minus fifty without a fire. He had trained for months in conditions like this. But this girl would probably die out here in the cold if he didn't find her soon.

The storm circled above them and around them. The trail had all but disappeared, except for the low glowing outline of the slope that led back up to it. Other than the white drifts that were blown from one place to another, the storm ushered in no new snow…yet. There was still some visibility, and if Kyle was going to do something, it had to be now. He listened to the palpitations of the storm. Like everything around him, it was alive, and its heart beat in a steady rhythm.

The storm breathed in: one…two…three. And out: one…two…three. Between the next break in the wind, he peeked over the log and looked for the place where the cabin should be. He thought for sure he'd see a square-like shadow somewhere in the distance, hinting the cabin's location, but he saw nothing. It didn't matter though. He had to try.

He looked at the dogs and yelled a familiar command. "Stay!"

Kyle almost laughed at the ridiculousness of his situation, but if they didn't listen to this one command, they could die. Or worse, he could. It was that simple.

The wind lashed alongside them, and he counted. *One...two...three.* It calmed, and he stood up, took several steps forward, and braced himself. It wasn't a heavy wind like a boxer's left hook. Instead it stung him with quick, glancing jabs. He abandoned the counting and waiting to move between the storm's beats, and he just ran.

His heart raced and his lungs burned as he swallowed the frigid air, but he pressed forward. It felt like he was moving as fast as he'd ever moved before. But any onlooker of the forest probably wondered why this man had decided to take a leisurely stroll in the midst of a storm.

Kyle would have never even seen the cabin if the wind hadn't hurled a piece of it right at him. He couldn't duck fast enough, and the broken timber rammed into his shoulder. He didn't know what hurt worse—the burning slap of the flat wood against his shoulder or the banging thud that ricocheted off his forehead. He thought back to Kallik's injuries. For a moment the world spun, or he spun—it was hard to tell which—until he tripped over something solid and hit the ground.

The land wasn't soft like he would have anticipated. It wasn't filled with powdery white snow or dirt. No, what he fell on was as hard as the board that had pounded into him. Because it was. Kyle looked around at the scattered objects. Pots and

147

pans, a couple jugs of gasoline or some other fuel, a shovel, and a makeshift chair. He felt the ground below him and realized it wasn't ground at all. He was laying on the side of the cabin, or at least what was left of it. And neither Faith nor King were anywhere in sight.

He tried to whistle, but the wind beat it down like a furious pugilist. Kyle pulled his parka hood tight around his face and tried to scan the edge of the forest, where they may have taken shelter. Nothing. No movement except what the wind shifted. Every sound was drowned out by the incessant wail that touched down all around him. Kyle abandoned reason and instead did something he hadn't done since he was a boy and King was a pup. He howled.

24

FAITH AND KING rushed out of the open field and into the cover of the forest's green-and-white fir. Her steps were sure and swift as she ran through her endless backyard. To their right, not more than twenty yards away, she had felled her first tree with her father. She leapt over a fallen log filled with pronged markings, where her mother taught her to shoot a bow. They passed by a mound of dogbane covered in snow, where she first learned to make rope with her bare hands.

She knew this land better than the sky above. Even in the growing blizzard, even as the winds knocked her from side to side.

King matched each of her steps with an easy trot. Ice stalactite hung from his nose and mouth. Crystals of frost were stapled to his ears and above his eyes. As Kyle had commanded, he stayed with Faith. Whether she turned right or left, it did not matter. Until they stepped out onto a frozen lake.

Faith didn't know if it was the feel of the sticky ice beneath them or the reexposure to the furious wind. But the dog that had ran by her side stopped.

He turned around and held his head firm in the air. The icicles on his nose twitched as he sniffed. One ear moved alone, unconstrained by the other.

Faith looked down the path that led back to the cabin, back to her house, decimated by the storm. A faint sound rose atop the wind and then died. And then it returned again. She looked across the lake to the abandoned cabin she had been running to for shelter and then back to King. She nodded and knew that their time together had come to an end. *Goodbye*, she said silently. And they both departed in opposite directions.

* * *

Back at Central, Jenna watched Kallik rock his little girl to sleep. He sat slouched in a chair with one hand on his wife's leg and the other holding his daughter to his chest. This man had experienced all the worst emotions of life in the past few hours alone. And now he waited, yet again, for a man he didn't know to come marching back to Central with his daughter, in the midst of an unyielding storm.

She caressed the skin between the ears of Duo, one of Ewan's dogs. Jenna's eyes had been fixed upon the door for the past couple hours. There were thirty-seven screws and nails that held the door together. She had counted, trying to take her mind off Kyle.

Duo lifted his head off her lap and growled.

"It's okay," Jenna said, doing her best to calm the dog. But not a single person at the checkpoint was calm. Not in this storm. Not with Kyle out there...alone.

Something cracked against the far wall, near the door, and several other dogs shot up. "It's all right," Jenna said. "It's all right."

Duo barked at another noise that came from the door. This time it sounded like a branch might be caught against it, scratching back and forth, back and forth.

Jed stopped fiddling with the radio and stood up from the booth. He stared at the door and scratched his head.

"What is it?" Jenna said.

"I...I don't know. I thought I heard something," he said.

Jenna stood up and walked over to him. There it was again. She lifted the latch, and the wind blew the door wide open. Snow shot into the room, followed by a broken tree branch. But behind it sprang a wind-beaten and snow-covered dog. Black like the night bounded into the room.

The dog ran along the adjacent wall, where they had sat the night before, and sniffed furiously. He reared up on his hind legs, his forepaws landing flat on the table where Kyle had slept.

Ewan's dogs barked and yipped, but King ignored them. He stopped in front of Jenna and looked at her, studying, searching.

She saw the pain etched into his eyes, the distress depicted in his every move as he searched for his friend, for his family.

Jenna sniffed back the tears and choked out the words. "Kyle isn't here, boy." He looked at her and let out a high-pitched whimper from behind his closed mouth. His eyes scanned the room one more time, but before Jed could close the door, King turned on his hind legs and bolted back out into the blistering storm.

Jed forced the door closed as the shadow of King disappeared like a dream.

"Why didn't you grab him?" Jed said. "You just let that dog go back out there?"

Jenna wiped her eyes before the tears became visible and walked back toward Ewan's dogs, ignoring Jed.

"Jenna, why didn't you grab him?" Jed said again in disbelief. "Wasn't that Kyle's dog?"

151

Ewan called out from the corner of the room. "That wasn't Kyle's dog."

Jed looked confused. "What do you mean? That was his lead dog. The one that was missing."

Ewan shook his head. "I've been around dogs my entire life. That wasn't a dog. That was a part of Kyle himself. A piece of his soul. And there isn't a single thing Miss Jenna, or anyone for that matter, could do to stop him."

"To stop him from what?"

Ewan put the knife down that he was using to pick the dirt from underneath his nail, and looked up at Jed. "From anything that separates him from Kyle."

25

KYLE HOWLED again and waited. To the north, back up near the trail, he heard a sound. It was unfamiliar, and almost sounded like...like someone dragging something heavy across the snow.

A few seconds later, Story's and Ria's heads broke through the cloak of falling snow that blocked his view. And behind them ten other dogs followed, dragging the sled with them. Everything inside Kyle wanted to smile as Story stopped the team in front of him, even though they hadn't obeyed his command. To make matters worse, the canvas pack that contained his supplies had ripped. His food, the dogs' food, his sleeping bag, extra coats and booties for the dogs, waterproof matches, hay—all of it was strewn about, scattering in the wind. And what didn't blow away was quickly covered by new snow.

The storm picked up again, and snow fell from the sky in thick white blankets, as if the clouds themselves were falling. Kyle lay on his side, Story licking the flakes from his face, while the wind howled through his wet clothes. Without King it felt like they were standing alone on the top of a mountain, just waiting for the storm to take them. He knew he only had one choice. While the trail was still visible, he had to turn back. But to his right, the opposite way, he spotted a trail that led into the woods. He surveyed all around him. If he were King, that was where he would have gone. Into the cover of the forest. Though every thought shouted to head back to Central, Kyle knew he wouldn't. He couldn't. So he flipped the sled upright, ignored the supplies that now belonged to the storm, and let the dogs pull him straight toward a switchback and out of the open.

The roaring storm drowned his commands in screams and shrieks. The forest felt fearful, alive. A giant sledge of sound cracked against Crazy Mountains behind them, and the dogs went berserk.

"Easy! Easy, Story!" Kyle yelled.

Even if they could hear him, they weren't listening. He jammed his knee down on the bar brake, and the sled slowed, but it didn't stop. Story and Ria pressed the team forward. Their unquenched desire to pull combined with the panicked pace of the storm created a recipe for disaster. This was why he paired Link with Story and Artemis with Ria. It was too late for that though.

In strong winds, leaders tended to turn downwind if visibility was bad or they didn't have a distinct trail to follow. It was the easiest way to get turned around on a trail.

The team banked past the broken back of a recently fallen tree, and the sled lurched off the ground as they sped over a series of moguls. There were many golden rules in mushing, and one was never let go. The dogs didn't know when to stop running, especially if they were spooked. Kyle gripped the sled so hard he thought he could feel the wood bend below him like warm clay.

"Easy, Colossus! Easy, Olympia!" he called again, hoping his wheel dogs would slow the team. Story and Ria would have

154

none of that. They wanted out of the storm. The harnesses tied them in, and every fiber of their being screamed to break free. This was the character of a great sled dog. The will, the drive. It was also the danger.

Kyle knew six-hour runs on the official trail, at approximately eight miles per hour, would generally get him to some type of shelter, be it a checkpoint, open cabin, or a good camp location. But how long had he been running, and how fast? He was in a storm, and worse, he was lost, chasing after some intuition to find King and Faith that would probably get him killed first.

The brush bow on the front of the sled crashed down hard against the ground, and the team shot out of the backwoods and back onto an open expanse. Kyle heard a metallic snap, and the aluminum brush bow kinked to the right. Blowing gales assaulted them from each side, and the bridle that held the dogs to the sled swayed and then jerked the sled forward awkwardly. Kyle was thrown down to one knee as his left leg shot out to the side, sliding along the ground, but something had finally slowed the dogs.

He waited for the sled to steady and pulled himself back to his feet. In front of him, on the side of him, behind him, was nothing but swirling silver ash. Through the blaring whiteout, Kyle couldn't see past Link and Artemis, the second pair of dogs in front of the sled. It wasn't until he looked down that he realized what had slowed the sled.

The runners and subrunners that the sled skated on were intact. Below them he watched patches of ice and snow drift by, but in between were long runs of translucent blue. He listened to the sled blades scrape across the ice. This wasn't dry ground. This was a lake.

"Easy, Story! Easy, Ria! Whoa! Whoa!" He continued to press the brake down so hard he thought it might snap right off the sled. He grabbed the claw brake that hung from the vertical frame by his left hand, ready to toss it behind the sled as well, but it was too late. The ice didn't crack all around him, giving him time to make a decision. It didn't warn him with easy groaning or trembling. It just broke.

Ice splintered around him and radiated outward several feet. The front of the sled cocked back like the hammer of a pistol and balanced on the edge of the break, where the ice was thicker. It jerked the dogs back and halted their furious rush. Colossus screamed out and kicked at the coarse lake snow. The rest erupted with a cacophony of yelps and barks, not sure why they were being dragged backward. The ground blizzard didn't relent, whipping drift snow and rime across their sides.

Water swallowed Kyle's feet and grasped at his legs. The sled teetered with him on one side and the dogs on the other, and then dipped down farther as he held on to the handlebars. His adrenaline was no match for the freezing water. It felt like someone was roasting his legs over an open fire, and the water sapped his lungs and reached out for his breath.

Another chunk of ice below the runners broke off, and the sled shot almost straight toward the sky. Water swirled around his waist and soaked past his skin to some place deeper.

"Hike, Story! Hike!" Kyle screamed. There was no breath to expel the words, and they came out like a whisper. For a moment he was almost eye level with the dogs' feet. He watched them scramble, the traction patches on the bottom of their booties barely keeping them moving.

They had run one of the hardest races in the world for the past ten days, and yet he watched them push ahead. He couldn't see Story or Ria, but he could see Colossus and Olympia, their massive hind legs driving forward. He could see Link and Artemis, their entire strength coming from the experience of their old age as they lowered their bodies against the weight.

The sled lifted up, and water dripped off Kyle's waist and froze to his suit. Once inch, two inches, five inches. They pushed forward.

"Come on!" Kyle said. His hands had never hurt so bad in his life. It felt like he gripped the sled with bare bones. "Come on!"

The lake was not yet finished. Just as his body started to rise from its wintry mantle, the lake sacrificed another section of its frozen sheath, and the sled dropped back down. Colossus and Olympia slid backward, toward the water that laid claim to Kyle's life.

He watched the team struggle against the inevitable, their feet searching frantically for a solid hold. Artemis, the old man of the team, slipped underneath the unforgiving weight and screamed out as his right side collided with the glacial surface. His voice cut through Kyle sharper and more painful than any affront the lake could offer. For a moment the wind only whispered, and Story's black head appeared beyond the floating snow. Her eyes locked on to Kyle's, distraught and demoralized by the immovable sled. It wasn't just Kyle's dead hanging weight that stalled them. It was the wind, the ice, and the blades of the sled positioned in such a way that they would have to pull it through the ice.

They couldn't do it. Even with King that would prove to be an impossible task. A task that might consume all their lives if he continued to hold on. So Kyle did the one thing he knew to never do.

157

He let go.

The sled stuck for a second, anchored in the edge of the fragmented ice. And then it launched forward.

Kyle didn't kick. He didn't thrash his arms about. He just let the water run arctic wash over him. Its crystal-blue hands pulled him down...down...until everything around him was dark. Black like a starless night. Like...King.

Kyle focused on that last thought. And like a candle first lit, an energy like a flame ignited. He shook off his gloves and kicked his legs with every last bit of effort he had in him. The air felt warm on his face when his body broke through the water's surface. He couldn't feel his hands all the way up to his shoulder, but he threw them like claws toward the rim of blue ice. They hit something hard, and he tried to hold on, but there was nothing.

Something moved in front of him as he sank back into the numbing waters. His ears were ringed with water, but he heard an approaching click below the ice.

Bwhoom, bwhhom, bwhooom. And then the noise slid across the ice and came to a stop.

This was it. He had nothing left in him. Several inches below the water felt like several miles. All he could do was cast his frozen arm up one last time. Like an anchor tossed among a bed of rocks, this time his deadened arm hit something.

Kyle tried to close his hands around it but couldn't even feel his fingers to know if they flexed. Still he tried. Higher, higher. His arm was moving out of the water. Slowly, but it moved. The water spilled off the sides of his face, and he gasped for breath. Steam rose around him where the blood of his once warm body mixed with the cool winds. A second trapped in the frozen water was a minute, and Kyle gasped again, his body starved from oxygen. Higher still his body continued to rise. The water broke free from his eyes, and he looked up to see two hands wrapped around his.

He looked up to see Faith.

26

WHEN KYLE OPENED his eyes again, he was shivering
inside a firelit room, weighed down by the familiar scent and
feel of black and ginger fur. He tried to move, but even his
thoughts were fraught with an embedded cold.

Ria's tongue felt like sunny water as it swept across his face.
Her body stretched atop him from his legs up to his chest. Her
warmth became his warmth. Another dog moved near his head.
On the ground behind him, the white tip of Story's tail wriggled,
and he felt her nuzzle against him. Link and Artemis spanned
the space along his left side, Colossus and Olympia the right.
Spirit and Shyanne, Hali and Sunshine, Gardens and Giza filled
the space in between. Some of them curled motionless, like
cotton balls. Others lay on their side or forelegs. All watched
Kyle.

The door to the barren room opened, and down dropped
a pile of firewood. Most of it dead and splintered spruce. Kyle
turned his head and saw the soft-spoken girl from before. The
girl who had been left not once but twice to wait for help.

Kyle had lots of questions. *How? Where are they? What
happened? Where is King?* But all he could manage for now was,
"Thank you."

Faith stacked two pieces of the fresh wood on the fire and nodded. "Get some rest."

The room filled with reinvigorated heat as the fire sated itself and consumed the dead branches. Ria laid her head down on his chest, just inches from his face, and Kyle let sleep take him.

* * *

Back at the checkpoint, Jenna stood by the door to Steese's. To everyone's dismay, she cracked it open every few minutes to see if the storm had subsided. To see if maybe Kyle was racing back toward her.

Several feet of windswept snow splashed into the room, and Jenna slammed the door shut.

Jed and Ewan whispered something from across the room, and then Ewan walked over to her. "Come. Sit down."

"I'm fine here," she said.

"You're driving everyone crazy," Ewan said.

"Don't beat around the bush any, do you?"

"Not usually."

"Just a few more minutes," Jenna said.

Ewan glared at her.

She pulled her hand from the door and lifted her weight off its frame. "Okay, okay. I'll stop." Only seconds had passed, and she already wanted to open the door one more time. Maybe Kyle had just broke the trail out of the woods and she'd see him in the far. Instead she followed Ewan over to his dogs. Solo looked up at her with restless eyes, and she sat down next to him.

"Don't give me that look," she said. "You know you'd be looking too if the shoe was on the other foot."

The dog exhaled a quiet groan and rested his head on her legs.

"He's still out there," Jenna said. "He has to be."

* * *

Faith was staring at Kyle when he opened his eyes for the second time. Ria had moved off his chest and was sitting next to Faith, but sprang toward Kyle at his slight movement.

Oomph. She just about knocked the wind out of him as she rolled up on her side and pressed her body against him. Her head flipped all around in excitement, and her tongue darted left and right.

"Okay, okay," Kyle said. "Calm." Ria spun onto her stomach and laid her head down next to him. Every bit of her was still except for her tail, which whirred like a propeller.

Kyle leaned forward and sat up. The long coat that covered his body slid down and exposed his bare chest. He wasn't cold—if anything, he was a little too close to the fire. But he was missing his shirt. He lifted the coat up and looked down toward his waist. In fact, he wasn't wearing anything.

He looked over at Faith, and for the first time he saw her smile. She looked down at the ground, trying to hide it behind a blushed face. "I'm sorry," she said. "But..."

"Don't be," Kyle said.

Faith stood up and placed her hand along Kyle's clothes that were hanging from a makeshift roast above the fire. She pulled them off the sticks and handed them down to Kyle. "They're pretty dry."

There were several wet spots on his shirt, but they were also still warm from the fire.

"How long have we been..."

"I'm not sure," Faith said. "Maybe four or five hours."

"Where exactly is here, by the way?" Kyle said.

"Are my mother and sister okay?" Faith said, not answering Kyle's question.

"I'm sorry," Kyle said, forgetting she didn't know. He saw her expression at the sound of his words and corrected himself. "No, I mean, they're fine. Jenna and Jed are looking after them right now. And your father is there too. If anything, they're probably just worried about you right now."

Faith ran her hands over her arms and let out a subtle shiver. She looked around the room and answered Kyle's original question. "We're a couple miles south of the mountains. This is a friend's place. But they're never here in the winter."

Kyle scrutinized the room. It was simple. Square. There was a bench hewn from several logs in one corner, with a tackle box or tool box below it. Probably nothing more than a summer hunting cabin, he thought.

"And the storm?"

"It's still out there."

"Are you hurt?"

"Not a scratch," Faith said.

A burst of wind engulfed the cabin, and it groaned like an old man getting out of bed in the morning. Kyle's thoughts flashed back to the flattened structure that Faith once called home. To the cast-iron kettle sitting above the shattered stove. To the makeshift chairs and hand-built beds toppled and torn. To the snowmobile cracked in half by a frozen tree. To the last place he saw King.

"I'm assuming you and King got split up in the storm?" Kyle asked.

Faith drew back her hood that hid her face like a fur-covered awning. She looked different, exposed, highlighted by the shifting light of the fire. Stunning was the first word that came to Kyle's mind. Maybe sixteen or seventeen, and every feature both smooth and stark. She locked eyes with Kyle.

"There was a noise," she started. "When we reached the lake. Behind us, I think. It was hard to tell. The wind was shooting past in screaming bursts. But when King heard it, he stopped. I looked back at him…"

She stopped recounting the story and said, "Don't think I'm crazy, but…even in the storm, I could sense something in him. Every part of him conveyed this indescribable knowing. It was just a few seconds, but I kind of thought he was apologizing. Like he had to leave, he had to answer the call, but he wanted me to know he was sorry for doing so."

Again Kyle thought back to just a few hours ago. Kneeling in the snow. King and Faith missing. Discouraged, distraught. "It's my fault."

"What is?"

"That King's gone." Kyle rubbed his hands over his eyes and realized they were a lot colder than he felt. He blew into them and scooted a few inches closer to the fire. "That noise that King chased after, that was me."

Faith looked at him, confused. "I don't think so," she said. "It sounded more like a wolf howling."

"I didn't know what else to do," he said. "I found the cabin collapsed, and both of you were gone."

Faith smiled. "So you howled?"

Kyle laughed. "Well, when you put it like that, it sounds kind of stupid."

164

"No, I mean, it's just an interesting choice," she said, joining him in laughter.

It felt good to smile, to exult in something. It was like sleep for the soul. Renewing. But as Kyle thought about King, it was also sad. "It was something we used to do when I was younger. We used to sit together at night and just stare up at the stars. And for some reason, I thought dogs were supposed to howl. King didn't have a mother or father, so I figured I'd teach him."

Faith leaned forward and listened.

"I'm sorry," he said. "I'm not sure why I'm telling you any of that."

"No, I like it," she said. "My father used to tell me stories like that. It's...nice."

Still, as he observed the dogs, it only reminded him of King's absence.

"King will be okay," Faith said plainly.

"I know," Kyle said. He felt a pressure on his arm and looked back to see Faith's hand clasping his shoulder.

"No, you don't," she said.

Kyle tilted his eyes up toward hers. They stood firm like two blue mountains.

"King will be okay," she repeated.

Chills shot through his arm and turned circles in his stomach until they settled firmly just above his heart. *Who is this girl?*

Story stretched her neck and propped her head on the backside of Ria. They both lay single file between him and Faith.

Artemis scooted between Faith's outstretched legs. Kyle noticed she had an easy way with the dogs. An unassuming alertness. She wasn't obsessed with their presence, constantly petting them. Rather, she was aware of their company and let her mental energy speak in the unseen language of animals. And the dogs spoke back.

Olympia eased up along her right side and nudged Faith's hand that rested on the ground. Faith laid it atop the dog's mixture of ginger-and-vanilla fur. Colossus loped over and groaned at Olympia. He had been perfectly comfortable resting closer to the fire but never liked to be apart from his sled mate.

"That's rare," Kyle said.

Faith relaxed against the wall. "What is?"

"The way you are with the dogs."

She looked down at her hand that gently stroked up and down Olympia's thick fur. "There's something different about these dogs," she said. "I can't really put my finger on it. But it's...something. They don't look like huskies. Are they a crossbreed?"

Kyle shook his head.

"Malamutes?"

Again, no.

"Wolf hybrids?"

"Perhaps years ago. Now they are Carolina grays," Kyle said.

"As in North Carolina?" she said in disbelief.

"As in South," Kyle said.

"You drove to South Carolina to get dogs?" Faith asked.

"Other way around."

"Dogs drove to South Carolina to get you?"

"I'm from South Carolina. I drove up here with the dogs about six months back to train for the Yukon Quest."

"So besides trying to drown yourself in half-frozen lakes, why on earth did you do that?"

166

Kyle didn't respond.

"Too soon?" she asked with a grin.

"Just a little." Kyle chuckled.

The cabin fended off a frosty gale that snuck through the vertical boards and tickled the fire. The storm boomed behind the wind, as if it were laughing with Kyle.

Kyle reached over and grabbed Faith's parka that had covered him earlier. He handed it to her.

"Thanks." She wrapped it around her. "But seriously, how? Why?"

Kyle thought about the question. He knew the answer. He felt the answer. He had just never put it into words. Even Doc hadn't asked him why before Kyle left. And when Kyle asked Doc if he wanted to know, Doc simply said, "This is your trial, not mine." And that was that.

The words came to him slowly. They formed like clouds, and the longer he stared at the words, the more they took shape. He pushed aside the feeling to hide part of the truth that might sound foolish, and just spoke.

"You know, I look at King. I look at the other dogs like Story and Ria and Colossus. I look at the way they see the world, the way they cause the world to react to them, instead them reacting to the world. They were born for this."

"I like that answer," Faith said. "But what about you? Why are *you* here?"

Kyle looked around at the dogs spread across the floor. He looked at his family. "What about me?" he said. "What was I born for? What if the answer is just average? What if my story was never meant to be unique? What if everything I believe in turns out to be wrong?"

Faith answered Kyle before he could answer himself. "What if the world does its worst to you, and when the dust settles, and the way clears, what if you're still standing? I don't know you. But I've watched you. I've seen your eyes. I've seen your stride. I've heard your song, just as the forest has. You're story isn't average. You're not average, and you don't believe that any more than you believe those dogs aren't your brothers and sisters. Your deepest fear is not that you are inadequate. Your deepest fear is that you are powerful beyond measure, but you won't do anything with that power. The funny part is you've already done more than most people ever will. The way you stand among the dogs like a sunset hovering over the ocean, providing endless light and warmth. To sway the very soul of the dogs. That is your gift. And because people twenty years from now, or fifty years from now, or one hundred years from now may not remember you, you continue to search. All the while you forget that right here, right now, the dogs remember you. My mother, my sister, my father, they'll remember you." She paused. "I'll remember you."

Kyle didn't move, but on the inside his mind couldn't comprehend how a sixteen-year-old girl raised in the Yukon could speak with such eloquence. Such truth.

"Seriously, who are you?"

"What do you mean?" Faith laughed.

"I mean I've never heard anyone talk like that. They just...don't...talk like that."

"I do," she said with a smile.

There was a brief lull in their conversation, and Sunshine stretched her dappled legs and groaned.

"Somebody's tired," Faith said.

"I think they're probably all a little tired," Kyle said. "Can I ask you a question?"

"Well, I had so many other plans tonight, but I guess I can make room for some questions," Faith teased.

"Your father," Kyle started. "Kallik. He's Inuit?"

"Full-blood Inuit," Faith said, nodding.

"But your mother is…"

"White," Faith said.

"And you guys have always lived out here?"

"Hopefully, not anymore," she said. "But yeah, we always have."

"You don't like it?"

"I hate it. Only two more years though, and I'll be out of here."

"What do you parents think about that?" Kyle said.

"My father is still under the delusion that I'm going to follow in his footsteps and never leave. My mother pretty much knows I'm leaving and not looking back." She paused. "Why?"

"I don't know," Kyle said. "Just making conversation."

"Well, what about you? Do you like South Carolina?"

"Yeah, it's nice. I live in a small farm town with my uncle and the dogs. I can't complain."

"So you're looking forward to getting back?"

Kyle thought about home. About some of the younger dogs that Doc was looking after. About the work he needed to do around the barn and the garden. Doc had become convinced that he'd invented a new manure using the dog waste, that grew plants even faster. He missed Doc, and yet even with all that had happened, he felt more alive now than he ever had.

He thought about waking up in the loft above the dogs to the faint scratching of King at the bottom of the ladder. The

169

scratching sound grew louder in his mind, grating and grinding so heavy it felt like it was coming from within the cabin. Kyle's eyes moved toward the door, and he shot up from his seat. Story and Ria sprung up, and then the rest of the dogs. Kyle ripped open the door, and the wind joined the dogs in a chorus of barks.

Standing in front of him was just a broken branch caught in the snow, rubbing its limbs against the cabin. Scratching. Grating. Grinding.

Kyle stared out into the dark storm and shielded his eyes from the biting wind. Everything stirred, and yet nothing moved. *I know you're out there, boy. Stay strong.* He shut the door, and Faith was standing behind him.

She didn't say a word but, in the same wisdom from before, stepped forward and hugged him.

27

THE YUKON WAS quiet when Kyle woke. Faith was still curled up with Olympia, her hands clinching at the dog's white fur, like a pillow. The fire had nearly burned down, and just the blackened wood coals flickered and simmered.

The dogs stirred as Kyle peered out the cabin door. During the darkness of the storm, it had been hard to tell whether it was daytime or nighttime. But right now he watched the morning sun cascade through the trees like stairways from heaven. A couple feet of fresh snow lined the forest, but other than that, no one would have even known a massive blizzard had passed through here.

Kyle held his hand, like a visor over his eyes, and searched deep into the woods. There were no tracks, no movement, and still no King. He pulled the door shut, and Faith sat up behind him. She yawned and tried to wipe the sleep from her eyes.

"Morning, sleepyhead," Kyle said.

"The storm?" she asked.

"Gone."

Her face lit up.

"Whaddya say you and I go for a little sled ride?"

"Only if you promise to avoid any lakes."

Kyle didn't respond.

"Still too soon?" she said.

"I'll just have to make sure I keep an eye on my clothes. They seem to go *missing* when I'm around you…"

"You. Wish."

They both laughed.

"All right, well, give me a few minutes to get the rigging all set up, and we can head out."

Faith threw her arms around the fluffy white dog next to her. "Okay, Olympia and I may get a little more beauty sleep."

"You need it," Kyle said.

"Hey!"

Kyle put his hands up. "Just a joke." He ducked out of the door as a piece of firewood clanged against it.

"Women," he said.

"I heard that!" Faith shouted.

Kyle laughed as he walked over to the sled. Faith had tied it solidly to a tree. The rigging was in knots and mostly buried, but it would be fine to make it back to Central. The sled, on the other hand, didn't look that great. The brush bow had cracked in half and was all but worthless. Two of the stanchions that pressed against the tree were also damaged. Nothing a little duct tape wouldn't fix, except for the fact that he didn't have any duct tape.

Both of the runners looked fine, which was the most important part, except for the right side footboard. It had been splintered in two. Kyle pressed his right boot against the remaining half. It wasn't ideal, but he could get by with that for several miles. He'd have to repair it before searching for King.

Kyle walked back into the cabin and found Faith, true to her word, cuddled back up with Olympia.

"Colossus," Kyle called. The giant teddy bear of a dog sauntered over to him. He bent down and rubbed the chunky fur behind his head. "You ready, boy?" Kyle walked him outside and clipped him into the sled.

Faith wasn't too happy when he called Olympia next. Faith got up and walked outside with Kyle. Her warm breath collided with the crisp air and created a cloud of condensation. She pulled the hair band off her wrist and arched her back, her long hair falling behind her and the outline of her body pressing against her clothes.

"What?" she said to Kyle, who was staring at her.

"Uh, nothing. I'm going to grab Artemis."

"Okay, I'm going to use the little girl's room."

"Don't stray too far," Kyle said.

She headed toward a few trees behind the cabin and called over her shoulder. "Okay, *Dad*."

Kyle moved back to the door and called out Artemis. "I don't know how you handle all these girls," he said to the old dog.

His team consisted of eight females and five males, including King. Artemis yawned and stretched backward with his tail in the air.

"You got that right," Kyle said.

He clipped him into his harness, tug line, and neck line. And then the worst possible thing happened.

Out of the clearing stumbled a calf.

28

THE TRAIL WAS full of dangers. Wolves, fox, jumble ice, steep and unkempt trails, dog injuries and illnesses, exhaustion, and even the sheer cold. But above all else, the one thing every musher feared most was a moose.

At first Kyle mistook the calf as a common deer. Its coffee-colored coat and bare face loped through the snow. But it didn't move with the grace and swiftness of a deer. Its pace was labored and clumsy. It was a young moose, rare at this time of the season. No more than a few months old, and completely oblivious to Kyle and the dogs.

The dogs' attention still traced after Faith's trail, and the fresh snow covered any sound from the ambling calf. Kyle froze in place. Where there was a calf, there was bound to be a cow, and possibly a bull. The animal kept moving, running about like a child at play. *Keep going*, Kyle thought. *Just keep going.*

A twig or leaf, or maybe just a clump of snow, cracked below the calf, and Colossus turned his great head and bellowed. Olympia and Artemis barked and leapt forward. The sled jerked but held because of the claw brake.

Turn. Please, just turn around.

The young moose was shocked by the sudden unfamiliar presence in his forest. Unlearned and unfinished by nature, the calf tripped over its own legs and stumbled toward the sled. It rolled twice and slid to a stop. Disoriented and scared, the animal climbed back to its feet but ran in the wrong direction.

Artemis had settled some, but Colossus and Olympia still screamed at the foreign animal. Kyle moved to pull the brake line, but it was too late. The young moose rambled through the snow where Kyle had stretched out the gangline. The calf tripped again over the vine of rigging and fell into several snow-covered bushes. Somehow, its back right hoof was racked and tangled in the lines. A strange cry of hees and haws echoed throughout the woods, and it kicked its legs frantically. Though just a few months old, the animal was still endowed with strength and jolted the same line Colossus, Olympia, and Artemis were tied too.

Kyle worked his way along the line, holding it with both hands as he moved toward the calf. One more kick though, and the line broke free. It whipped back at Kyle, and the shift in weight sent him falling backward, one of the neck lines lashing his face.

He breathed out in relief as the calf darted past them, chased away by the barking dogs, but it wasn't done. The animal continued to call out in distress as it ran, and twenty yards north of where Kyle sat, an antler appeared.

The full-grown bull stood over six feet at its shoulders. A single antler covered in velvet and snow clung to its right side, having likely dropped the other one recently. He had a massive barrow, a short tail, and long legs. Easily over a thousand pounds.

Kyle blinked. "This isn't happening. This isn't happening."

Faith ran around the corner. "What is going on?"

175

Kyle stood up slowly as the moose walked closer. "Get in the cabin."

"What?" Faith said.

"Now!"

It could have been his voice, or Faith's movement, the dogs' barking, or the calf still screaming. Kyle didn't know. But the moose broke into a full run directly at them.

Kyle pushed Faith toward the door and moved back to his dogs. He unclipped Artemis' neck line, but the moose reached the team before Kyle could do any more. The mighty animal reared back on its hind legs, head inclined, dewlap shaking, and stomped forward. Kyle rolled over backward, and Artemis leapt to the left, but the moose made no effort to avoid the dogs.

Its wide hooves dove down at the dogs, and Artemis screamed out with an unfathomable noise. It was guttural and growling, almost Jurassic.

In his peripheral vision, Kyle noted Faith opening the door to squeeze inside the cabin, and Artemis yelped again as he and the other two dogs scrambled to dodge the moose's hooves. Kyle surveyed behind him, from the side of the sled, and saw Ria emerge between Faith's legs. Faith closed the door behind her, but it was too late. Ria broke out, the rest of his team inside barking, unnerved, confined by the cabin.

The moose stomped through the team, tangled in the gangline, and dragged them into a huge ball. The bull paused for a split second, and Kyle reached for the basket of his sled. For his axe. The basket was empty though, and the axe was buried somewhere in the Yukon, from the night before.

Without warning the moose aimed its attack at Kyle and jumped over the sled. His single antler angled down like a bayonet, and he cleared the sled and stumbled into some deep snow around a tree.

Back and forth the bull tossed his great palmated head as he pulled himself to his feet.

Kyle sprang from his knees toward Ria and reached for her collar. He felt the coarse nylon fibers between his fingers for a brief second. And then she was gone. She was young like the calf. Unfinished. Unlearned. And in midair, just as her jaws were about to close on the beast, she received a shock that checked her body and brought her teeth together with an agonizing clip.

Ria looked back at Kyle and crumpled. She lay there limp and lifeless in the bloody, trampled snow.

"Noooooo!"

He jumped over Colossus and Olympia, moving toward his little girl. He ignored the moose. Nothing was in his sight except Ria's still body. He didn't see Faith running from the cabin. He didn't see the moose charging toward him.

Faith collided with Kyle just in time and knocked him from the bull's path. The animal's antler knifed right and sliced across Kyle's waist. He screamed out, but not before the antler swept back to the left and pierced Faith. She twisted, and her body flung into the tree behind her as Kyle fell to the ground. He rolled over once, and his foot caught on something hard. It stopped his momentum, but something snapped loudly in his knee.

Several feet away Faith slumped against the trunk of a tree. He tried to crawl forward, but his right leg gave out, and pain shot through his knee and up his hamstring. When he reached Faith, her deerskin parka was already soaked in blood. He pressed his hands over Faith's stomach.

"It's going to be okay," he said. "Just hang on!"

From behind them one of the dogs howled. A bloodcurdling howl.

And in the white, in the woods, in the wild, that howl was answered with something so heart wrenching and fierce, fear shivered through Kyle's body.

Out of the forest something moved. Swift like a river. Eyes of endless amber. Fur near midnight black. King bounded toward them with a relentless resolve.

Unlike the others, King was wild once. He wasn't putting on anything new. He was returning. Not just to Kyle, but to his feral beginnings.

The moose pivoted and reared its head to his right, where this new threat emerged.

King anticipated this and jolted right. His back legs sprang him forward as he left the ground, his body contorted until his feet met the wall of the cabin. Parallel to the ground, he pushed off the creaking timbers and slid to a stop in front of Kyle and Faith.

The snow shifted around his paws as King dug them into the ground and lowered his head. His hackles stood on end from his neck to his tail, giving him the appearance of being three inches taller and twenty pounds heavier.

The moose turned back on him and pawed his hoof, snorting hot breath out of his nostrils like a horse in the starting gates.

King let out the most base, feral growl Kyle had ever heard. The dog stared down the creature with a mental energy that seemed to move all of nature around him. As if to say, *you may have just been protecting your turf, but now I will protect my family.*

It happened so fast that Kyle didn't realize what had occurred. King moved. He moved in a way Kyle had never seen a dog move before, like a falcon diving from his kingdom of blue sky, or a sea lion racing around the Arctic Circle. King rushed at the moose, a blur of speed and grace, sinking his teeth into the animal's flank.

The moose cried out and flinched, falling back several feet. But King's attacks were unending. He feinted right several times and swept around the moose to the outside. His teeth clicked with ferocity. King had found gaps in the animal's armor of thick skin, and gashes of red began to appear across the moose's legs and flank. The bull began to learn King's tricks and tactics, but King was still faster. Hackles raised, lips curled, a dance of brilliance sparkled in his careful eyes.

This wasn't over though. The moose was savage in its survival. It shook free of King and initiated its own vicious attack. It stood almost still, its antler and barrow a shield, its hooves spears that launched forward and back. King took one of the hooves to his side and flew backward several feet.

Once down, that was the end of most dogs. But King wasn't most dogs. The facts of life took on a fiercer aspect; and while he faced that aspect uncowed, he faced it with the learned poise of nature's lethality.

Ears laid back, King circled. They traded a quiet and menacing glare, a ritual of those things born of the wild. It felt as if the Maker had switched off the air and chilled the very ground where the two stood in epic battle.

An ancient song that every man and animal once knew, surged through King. Slowly, at first, like the sound of footsteps marching from a distant place. He shook his head from side to side, bits of froth and slobber slung to the ground. The song beat louder, and something long dead in King sprang to life again.

He opened his mouth with neither bark nor bite, neither howl nor haw. The noise he made was more like a roar that shook the forest floor, and then he lunged.

The moose's black eyes glazed over as he saw defeat, and King's fangs bit down once again on the animal's sweet flesh. The bull's madness was quenched by King's ferocity, and the moose pulled back and bolted down the embankment behind the cabin, toward the calf.

King chased until Kyle called out, and the black dog trotted back to him, his muzzle framed in blood and sucking in the air around him. He stopped just inches from Kyle.

King had returned.

29

FAITH'S BREATHING slowed as she lay silent and still in the reddened snow. Her head hung loose, her eyes shut.

Kyle lifted her face in his hands. Her cool flesh burned against his. "Faith," he said. "Come on, Faith." He lifted her eyelids with his thumb. Only emptiness sat behind them. "Hang on."

He pushed himself to his knees and wrapped his arms underneath her and lifted her up. "Aaaghh!" Kyle screamed out in pain from the weight on his right knee. Even her lithe body was too much for him. He took a step with his left leg, but his right leg felt like stone cemented to the ground. The sled was only a few feet away. *This is going to hurt.* He forced his leg forward, and it flung out, lifeless and stiff. When it hit the ground, pain shot through his knee and up to the gash on his hip. A single tear contrived of involuntary pain dropped from his eye, and he screamed out again.

"Aaaghhh!"

Again he planted his left foot forward and drug his right, and again he screamed out in pain.

King barked, ordering him forward. Just one more step and he reached the sled, nearly collapsing on top of Faith as he set her into the basket.

He let himself fall to the ground and swung behind him to where Ria lay still as Faith. "Come on, girl," he said. "It's going to be okay." He rolled her up to his chest and then spun back around to the sled and rested her gently on Faith's lap. Neither moved.

King sat near Artemis and licked at the dog's peppered face. The gangline strung out and twisted to the left, where the calf had been tangled in it, and all Kyle saw were ten empty places. Several of the dogs barked from inside the cabin, behind the closed door, over twenty feet away. *I can't do this. I can't do this.* The words repeated over and over in his head until the desperation swelled and overcame the adrenaline that had coursed through his veins before. He moved his hand over his side, and fresh blood stuck to it like hot glue. He felt dizzy and lightheaded. *I can't do this.*

He looked at Faith and Ria, at Colossus and Olympia. At Artemis. At King. He heard Doc's voice in the back of his head echo louder than any other. *Get up, or give up. Get up. Or give up. Get. Up.*

Kyle wanted to stand more than anything he had ever wanted. But he'd need that energy to drive the sled. If he spent all of that energy just getting the dogs clipped in, there was no way he'd make it back to Central. So he clawed and dragged his body forward. He straightened out the gangline and glanced back at the cabin where the dogs remained. The last obstacle was the closed door. Story was still in there though. She could do this. She could push the door open from the inside. He knew she could do this. He knew she would answer his call.

"Story!" Kyle yelled, ignoring the jabbing pain in his stomach. "Come!"

The oak-filled door rattled. He could hear the dogs scratch at it. They pushed the frozen wood, and the door opened, but only a few inches before slamming shut.

"Story!" Kyle yelled again. "Come!"

He could hear her whimper and whine, unable to obey the command.

"Story! Come!"

The noise at the door stopped, and from the window he saw the pointed black ears and marble eyes. They searched until they found his and then disappeared.

Kyle prepared to call again. But before he could, a silvery crash shattered the silence of the Yukon. The wooden crossbars splintered, and the glass from the window exploded and scattered over the white floor. Story's body sprang through the air in a perfect line, her eyes closed, her ears laid flat. She landed on the forest floor and shook off the glass.

She ran up to Kyle, her face and nose scratched. A shard of glass was embedded in her cheek.

"Good girl," Kyle said as his swing dog licked his face. He pulled the glass from her cheek, and she let out a short whimper. "It's okay, girl."

Behind her followed seven others: Sunshine, Hali, Giza, Gardens, Spirit, and Shyanne. He pulled himself along the snow and clipped each of the dogs in place behind King. Only one dog remained, and he sat silent inside the cabin.

"Link!" Kyle called. "Come!"

Nothing. No scratch at the door. No ghostlike appearance where the window used to be. No whimper or bark. Nothing.

Link was a great dog. Fast, even keeled in the trace, smart. But he was also the most timid dog on Kyle's team.

"Link! Come!"

183

Kyle waited and watched the space near the broken window. "Come on, Link," he said to himself. "Come on."

Just as before, a crash echoed throughout the forest, but this time it didn't come from the window. The door boomed open and flung back against the cabin as Link shot out. He ran in a huge sweeping arc around the team, like something chased him, before circling back to his place next to Story and behind King.

"Good boy," Kyle said. He scratched the dog just above the tail. Every dog had a different spot of affection, and Link's just happened to be a good long butt scratch.

Once King was clipped in, Kyle fought his way on hands and knees behind the sled. The dogs didn't understand his awkward movements, and some yipped and jumped about as he passed, clearly thinking this might be some type of play. He ignored them though, focusing solely on pushing down the pain that coursed through his entire right side.

He used the handlebar to pull himself to his feet, and kept all his weight on his left foot. Instead of hanging the claw brake from the last vertical, he wrapped the extra line around his right hand, tying it to the sled.

"King," Kyle said. The lead dog looked back at him. "Lay hold. Leave nothing."

And in the quiet calm of a clear Yukon day, Kyle gave a command he hadn't given since he was a kid. "King, go home."

* * *

Breath upon breath the dogs built a pace that had never been matched. Not by the dogs of old that ran in front of the hard-handed whips. Not by any pack of wolves that stretched out across this land, muscles tensed to the edge of survival. No, the

Carolina grays, Kyle's dogs, ran on an edge that had never been approached.

People often asked themselves at one time or another, "Did I give my all? Could I have done more?" The dogs never even considered that question. This was their everything.

Kyle looked down at his stomach where his parka still soaked in a steady stream of blood. He tried to hold his right hand just under his last rib, where the antler had lacerated his side. But it wasn't enough. The dizziness returned.

He wasn't giving commands anymore. He had no energy to do so. King would lead them back. Kyle knew it. King would lead them back. He had to.

They careened around a left-banking turn, and the sled rails clipped the edge of a pine, flinging flakes of bark into the air. The jolt sent a stabbing pain across Kyle's midsection, but Faith didn't make a sound as her body jostled and shook with the wavering of the sled.

Standing behind the sled, Kyle couldn't see her face, but he yelled out anyway. "Faith! Just a little longer!

"King, hike! Hike!" Yelling like that sent a piercing pain through Kyle's side and chest. But still he urged the dogs onward.

Every fascia, every muscle, every fiber must have been failing. Their bodies, their bones, surely ached in the deep places and down to their hearts. Still the dogs pushed on, not by discipline or will, but because a man who loved them more than his own life asked them to. A man named Kyle Walker.

Nothing but the *whuuff* of the dogs' labored breath could be heard. All of nature watched the dogs work in a tacit silence. For nature was the only one to understand what was truly happening.

The dogs were tired. They were hurting. Their muscles ached, and their minds were restless.

Some said this was the moment a dog became almost human—when it exhibited a hint of sacrifice for others. But Kyle didn't ever make that mistake. Didn't insult the dog like that. Its whole was a sacrifice. It was in these moments of great sacrifice that man strove to be like the dog, not the other way around.

The sled reverberated off a dip and dive, only softened by the fresh snow from the storm. The shock of pain dropped Kyle to one knee, and if it wasn't for his right hand being tied to the handlebar, he may have fallen off. Between the rear stanchions, Kyle saw Artemis' head bob up and down next to an empty space where Ria normally ran, and the loss of Ria swept across Kyle's body.

He tried to shake off the feeling, to shut it out. But there wasn't enough adrenaline in the world to calm his broken heart. Several tears streamed down his face and dried instantly in the bitter headwind.

The tug line that connected Story's harness to the towline was tight, and there were times that Kyle thought it might burst from the sheer force of her effort. She looked over at Link, her tongue flopping from one side of her mouth to the other, and let out a rapacious rout.

King, never to be outdone, let loose a rich bark. He wasn't challenging her as much as cheering her on. *Run, Story. Step out of your domestic skin and into your ancestral past. Into the primitive. Into the unbroken ways of the wild. Run, Story. Run.*

30

THE STORM HAD dissipated by morning, sneaking out of the Yukon during the night. Other teams pressed on, even with the news of Kyle's disappearance. Frank Lesh was on his way to Two Rivers, probably halfway by now, but Jenna Maynor hadn't moved since first light.

She squinted into the collapsible binoculars, into the white horizon of the west. Sitting on one knee, alone, in front of Steese's Roadhouse, she saw nothing.

She regarded Ewan and his dogs, resting outside in reprieve of the past day spent inside. The sun beat down on the tundra, and even in zero-degree weather, some of the dogs scratched away their bed of straw, letting their bodies soak into the snow.

Without warning, his lead dog sprang up and released a series of howls. *Roo! Ru! Ruuuuuuuh!* The dog's ears perked, and he looked into the distance toward the southwest. A black speck crested a hill and transformed into a string of black and white. It moved with the rolling cadence of a freight train. The gangline bounced like a connecting rod, the dogs strode like pistons, and their heat rose off their backs like a smokebox.

She couldn't believe it. Kyle Walker had returned.

Ewan swung around from next to his dogs and looked back at Jenna. His frosty mustache wriggled as he spoke the same words repeating in her mind: "He's back."

They stood outside, side by side, staring into the coming hope.

She looked through the binoculars and then passed them back to Ewan. "I don't understand. Where did he go?"

"I don't know," Ewan said. "I saw him on the back of the sled—I swear. It looks like there's someone in the sled too. Maybe he stopped and hopped in the basket, knowing the dogs could take it from there. I don't know."

Mike's voice broke out over the radio. "Air to Central. Air to Central. We have visual on a sled team off trail and heading your way."

Jed responded. "Central to Air. We see them, and we have a team ready."

"Copy that, Central. I'll be putting down on your west side for transport."

"If needed," Jenna said to Jed.

"If needed," Jed said to Mike.

"Copy that, Central. If needed."

They watched and waited. What took only minutes felt like hours. The small rescue team that had assembled joined them. One man offered to meet them halfway on a snowmobile, but Ewan made a good point. That would just spook the dogs. So instead they watched until the sled glided closer, maybe fifty yards away.

One woman screamed out, and another man shouted. Several just gasped in horror.

"Kyle!" Jenna screamed. "Kyle!"

Huey stood silently next to her while another photographer started snapping off photo after photo, the electric clicks filling the space behind Jenna. She wanted to turn around and kick the camera out of the guy's hands, but she couldn't take her eyes off Kyle. King had brought him back, but his arm was lashed to the driving bow, as his lifeless body dragged across the snow.

31

Two Weeks Later

A TAN-COLORED phone rang in the kitchen. It vibrated along the wall and leaked a tinny sound throughout the trailer. Kyle stood on the steps, watching through the screen door.

Doc's calloused hands wrapped around the receiver, and a fingernail-size piece of paint chipped off.

"Heeello," Doc said. "No, no, he doesn't live here anymore... Yes, yes, that's what that last caller said." Doc chuckled. "And the caller before that... I'm not sure... Okay... You too."

He clicked the old rotary phone back to the hook switch.

Kyle swung open the screen door to the front porch. It rattled against the plastic trim.

"You got another call," Doc said.

Kyle set his crutch against the fridge and grabbed a water. "Was it her?"

"Why don't you just call her? She'll understand."

"Was it her?" Kyle said again.

"No, just another reporter looking for a musher that doesn't exist."

Kyle grabbed his crutch and slid the towel-wrapped support under his arm. He kicked open the screen door again and let it slam shut.

Doc caught the door with his bare hand and pressed it open as Kyle struggled down the front steps.

"Kyle," Doc said.

Kyle stopped on the dirt road in front of the house, but didn't turn around.

"Don't do this. Don't hide from this and shut everyone out. You couldn't have done anything more. You saved that woman and her daughter. No one, and I mean no one, could have done what you did."

Kyle turned around and faced Doc. He grimaced as he twisted and clutched at his side.

"You understand that, right?" Doc said.

"I failed that girl," Kyle said plainly. He pivoted around on his crutch, and a cloud of dirt kicked up around his feet.

"Kyle," Doc said. "Kyle, please."

But he just kept walking until the barn closed around him.

* * *

Kyle bit down on the water bottle, holding it tight in his mouth as he climbed the ladder to the barn loft. Each step sent a jounce of pain through his side, but he welcomed the throbbing that served as a reminder. He climbed over the final step and hobbled over to the table next to his bed.

He sat the water down on the desk and pulled a brown granular canvas-bound book out of the right desk drawer and opened it to several pages in. The words he wrote the night before stared back up at him.

What falls away is always and is near

The surest path is folly when unclear
No one escapes the white when it is wild
Not even the faithful voice of a child

What falls away is always and is near
The surest path is folly when unclear
No one escapes the storm's white wraith
Not even a girl full of faith

Kyle licked his finger and turned the page. And then he wrote down the first line again.

What falls away is always and is near

The words stung an unknown place within him. It wasn't a hole or a void, as some might describe it. No, something else. Something was missing within him. This had been his greatest fear. Something was lost, and it may never be found again.

Kyle pulled the elastic string over the book and tucked it back into the drawer. He descended the ladder down to the first floor of the barn, grabbed his crutch, and hobbled to the far end of the dusty kennel.

The latch on the last kennel gate jammed. He reached over to the tool table next to the gate, grabbed a can of WD-40, and doused the thumb latch in lubrication. It flicked open, and the jet-black dog that had been leaning against the gate stood up.

Kyle bent over halfway and rested his hands on his knees. "How you doin', girl?" he said.

The dog flicked her tongue over her lips and nose anxiously and sniffed at Kyle's hands.

"You want to try a little walk today?" Kyle asked.

The dog pushed her head between Kyle's legs, and he smiled.

"All right," Kyle said. "Nice and easy." He walked about ten feet away to the double barn doors, slung open.

The dog walked gingerly toward him, favoring her right side. Her head crested the final shadow of the barn, and she stepped through into the sun.

Kyle knelt next to the dog and traced his finger over the shaved skin on her side, past the row of stiches that felt like frayed leather. They curved in an ellipse, like the path of the sun, and stopped next to two freckles. Kyle hadn't won the Yukon Quest, but he knew their scars told a story of unceasing effort.

Ria stood next to Kyle, their silhouette highlighted by the morning sun, and he wondered if Kishkumen was still looking down from above. He wondered if Jenna would wake to find the same sky and the same thoughts.

"What do you think, girl?" Kyle said.

Ria sniffed at the aluminum crutch that supported Kyle's left side.

"You think we'll be okay?"

The young dog looked up at him, with black, pain-filled eyes.

"I know it hurts, girl. I think the journey always does."

END
OF
BOOK
ONE

A SPECIAL PREVIEW OF
HOPE IN EVERY RAINDROP
BOOK TWO OF FAITH, HOPE, LOVE

1

KATIE PRICE SET HER LAPTOP on the counter, the cursor still blinking on the blank page as she grabbed a pencil and her hardbound journal. She unlocked the double French doors that led to her back porch and pushed them open wide. The single hook screw groaned in the overhead beam as she settled into her hammock chair. She folded the cover of the journal over on itself and scribbled the date in the top right corner of the first page.

October 29, 2007

Then she did the same thing she had been doing all morning: she stared restlessly at the empty page in front of her.

It had been nearly six months since her father passed away, and she'd barely managed to write a single word in that time. It was the longest she'd ever gone without getting something down on the page.

Katie sat there until just before noon, staring out at the Pacific Ocean, the paper and pencil abandoned on her lap. From the back porch she could see almost all seventy miles of the San Diego coastline as it curved slightly toward Mexico around the Baja Peninsula.

The combination of the waves gently crashing on the beach and the slow sway of her hammock stilled her thoughts. Normally she would have reveled in the quiet, but she was restless and wanted more than anything to find her next story.

She pressed the lead tip of the pencil against the paper, hoping for that one word that would send her off into endless hours of writing. Nothing came except the interrupting chirp of her phone.

She eased herself out of the chair and set the pencil and journal on the counter next to her computer as she walked back inside. The screen on her phone lit up with a number that was all too familiar: her agent.

For a moment, she held the phone in her hand, thinking she might just slide the ringer to silent and take a walk on the beach. Or better yet, she could throw the phone on the ground and stomp on it until it shattered into a thousand tiny pieces. Unfortunately, she knew that wouldn't solve her problems. Not answering would just mean within a few hours her agent would pull into the driveway in her fancy BMW—if not today, then tomorrow or the next day. Katie didn't have any options.

"Hello, Samantha," Katie said, drawing out her full name in annoyance.

"Please tell me you've got something."

Katie halfheartedly tried to lie. "I've got something, Sam."

"Oh, Katie," Sam said. "What am I going to do with you? You can't even lie well lately. At least embellish a little, make up the name of your next lead character, or hint at some masterful plot you're still working out the details on."

Katie didn't respond.

"Still not writing, I take it?"

Katie let out a brief sigh as she stared back out at the water. "Not a word."

"Katie, you know I love you. You're my little prodigy. And while I know you're only twenty-one, you're playing in the big leagues now. Your publisher is breathing down my neck—if you don't come up with something in the next month, they're going to start requesting you return a portion, if not all, of the advance for this next book. I'll keep trying to cover for you, but with the economy the way it is…well, you know."

Again Katie didn't say anything. She just nodded, as if Sam were standing right in front of her with her fancy high heels and matching designer purse. Her agent's career had taken off after Katie's first couple of novels had made her the youngest woman on record with back-to-back bestsellers in the same calendar year.

"I don't mean to pry, but have you tried perhaps reading through some of your father's old work, to see if that might spark something?"

Katie reached down and picked up a dark-brown book with a title scrawled in gold letters. It was her father's first anthology of poems—the first literary work ever published under his name. It had never gained much traction with the public, but the poems had long been one of the reasons Katie had become a writer. His words always filled her with hope, and she had wanted so badly to pass that same feeling on to others.

3

She ran her hands over the lettering of her father's name on the spine of the book. Over the past few months she must have read each poem ten times, especially one he wrote for her.

Let the rain add to our tears
Until the day when all the pain has stopped
And we will say there was hope in every raindrop

To this day Katie would swear that her father was twice, even three times, the writer she was, but as a poet he never managed to find the success she had in fiction.

"I haven't, but maybe I'll try," Katie lied, this time convincingly.

"I think you should. I think that may help you find your voice again."

Katie walked toward the bookshelf behind her couch and started to speak again, but Sam cut her off.

"I'm sorry, hon, but I've got another call coming in that I have to take. I'll touch base with you in a week or so. We need to at least give them a sample to keep 'em busy. Remember, thirty days."

And with that Sam hung up.

Katie set her phone on the end table and pressed her father's book back in its place on the shelf.

"How did I ever write a *New York Times* best seller?" she said out loud. Her own books stared back at her. The stories had always come so easily before.

She turned to go back to the porch, forgetting about the boxes of her father's stuff she had stacked behind the couch.

As she moved, she stubbed her toe on the corner of one box and knocked over another that was next to it.

"Shoot," she said as she reached down to her foot.

When she stood, she realized that half the contents from the box she'd hit had spilled out across the floor. She knelt, starting to put them back in the box labeled "Dad's Stuff." Most of the contents were old journals or notes her father had made while drafting his books, and it didn't take her long to toss everything back where it belonged. But one object had slid about ten feet across the room.

It was a small wooden container about the size of a cigar box. There was a metal clasp on the front that held it shut and two hinges on the back that split it in two perfect halves. Nothing about the container looked familiar. In fact, Katie was pretty sure she had never seen it before.

A shiver ran through her body, and tears formed in her eyes as she unclasped the lock and opened it. Sitting on top was a small cross—actually, just two sticks tied together with twine. But underneath that cross was a photo of her mother. It was a small faded portrait, maybe two inches by three inches. The corners of the picture had started to peel away, and the glossy surface was beginning to crack.

She had seen this picture before, but not for a very long time. Not since she had finished her first novel.

Katie put the photo back down next to the cross and lifted out a gold-plated pocket watch with the name *Price* inscribed on the back. She didn't have to close her eyes to perfectly recall her father incessantly checking the watch and stuffing it back in his tweed jacket whenever he was stuck in his writing.

Below the watch, however, was an object she was sure she had not seen before.

Katie turned the folded piece of paper over in her hand. It wasn't normal lined paper. It had a familiar feel to it, except for the small bulge in the center. One side was taped to prevent it from unfolding. She used her thumbnail to gently peel back the tape.

As she opened it, she realized why it seemed familiar, though she was certain she had never seen this specific one. It was a map of the United States.

Katie pushed aside several boxes and cleared an area large enough to lay out the entire map flat on her wood floor. There were several pin-sized holes scattered across the surface. In the lower right corner, just above the legend, she found a dart held down by another piece of tape.

She removed the dart and set it aside, revealing several words written in cursive below it.

The ink was slightly faded, but she could still make out each word.

There are stories all around you if you only take the time to look.
Love always,
Katherine

Katie felt her body tremble again as tears streamed slowly down her cheeks and onto the map. She quickly ran her hands under her eyes, wiping away the tears, and tried to blot out the wet spots on the paper with the hem of her shirt.

Her mother must have given this to Katie's father before she was even born.

For a moment, Katie just stared at the beautiful handwritten words from her mother. Her eyes traced the sweeping arc of each letter as it ran into the next. She repeated the words again in her head, but her emotions clouded their specific meaning.

Her thoughts trailed off as her gaze returned to the silver dart lying next to her. The tip was sharp, and the body was rough as she ran her hand over it toward the three blue fins at the other end.

Then it all dawned on her.

Katie quickly grabbed the map and trotted to the kitchen, ignoring the pain in her stubbed toe. Opening a drawer, she grabbed a roll of scotch tape and walked out to her porch.

She turned to face the house, looking for a section of the wall large enough to hang the map. There was just enough room between two of the back windows. She taped the four corners, pressing the paper as close to the wall as possible.

She took several steps back with the dart in her right hand, imagining her father doing something similar all those years ago. But as she looked back at the map, something seemed wrong. She could make out the name of each state, and in many cases some of the cities that were printed in larger letters. Walking back over, she ran her hand across several places where she saw holes. Instead of feeling a smooth surface, she felt the punctured paper pressing out toward her. The dart couldn't have been thrown at the map facing this direction.

She set the dart on the handrail and removed the tape she had just placed on each of the corners. Then she turned the map over so the blank side faced her and again ran her fingers over the myriad of pinholes. Smooth.

Standing back at the edge of her porch, all she could see was a plain white piece of paper taped to her wall. Still, she could aim toward the center of the map and hit Missouri, Nebraska, or Kansas. Or for the corners and land on Florida, Georgia, New York, Maine, Washington, California, and so on. So she picked up the dart and turned her back to the map. Counting to three, she spun back around and let the dart go without hesitation. It wasn't a perfect throw, but it stuck solidly to the wall with a thud.

She pulled the dart from the wall, careful to reach around to the front of the map with one hand and mark the spot as she turned it over and set it on the porch floor. The small hole was in the dead center of a city she had never heard of in South Carolina.

The first drop of afternoon showers landed on the steps a few feet from her. Looking out again into the vastness of the deep-blue rolling waves, Katie couldn't help but feel excitement at the simple thought of one word.

Bishopville.

About the Author

Wesley Banks was born and raised in Bradenton, Florida. He graduated from the University of Florida with a bachelor's and master's degree in civil engineering. After spending over seven years building movable bridges from Florida to Washington, he decided to focus on his true passion: writing.

Wesley recently moved to Oregon to get back to the great outdoors that he loves so much. He lives with his wife, Lindsey, and his two dogs, Linkin and Story. Most of his time these days is spent writing, with as much rock climbing, hiking, or skiing as he can fit in.

Author Page: WesleyBanksAuthor.com

Note from the Author

I sincerely hope you have enjoyed reading this book as much as I enjoyed writing it.

If so, I would love for you to do two things:

1. Leave a review on Amazon telling what you loved about the book.
2. Come find me at WesleyBanksAuthor.com, and let's connect. I love catching up with my readers.

CPSIA information can be obtained
at www.ICGtesting.com
Printed in the USA
BVOW03s2143040417
480328BV00001B/66/P